THE LABYRINTH

WINNER
MILES FRANKLIN LITERARY AWARD
2021

WINNER
PRIME MINISTER'S LITERARY AWARDS
2021

WINNER
VOSS LITERARY PRIZE
2021

WINNER
TASMANIAN LITERARY AWARDS
2022

SHORTLISTED
AGE BOOK OF THE YEAR AWARD
2021

SHORTLISTED
QUEENSLAND LITERARY AWARDS
2021

'*The Labyrinth* is Amanda Lohrey's wisest and most intimate novel yet—luminous, full of sharp-edged beauty and illuminating questions about how we should live our lives. It asks, most simply, how to keep going in the wake of a disaster that has no neat ending. This is a novel in which nothing is out of place—every word and image resonates.' Julieanne Lamond, author of *Lohrey*

'A beautiful, brutal book that I experienced as both earthy and unearthly. I loved it.' Laura McPhee-Browne

'Hypnotic and beautiful, *The Labyrinth* forces us to reckon with how our deepest bonds can inflict the most pain. Amid this coil of darkness, however, is the novel's unfailing light: that hope and redemption are always found in art and creation.' Rebecca Starford

'Not a book to be analysed but a book to experience. It is compelling, visceral and deeply moving…It is delicate yet strong. Painful yet regenerative.' Fiona Place

'Beautiful…Quite possibly my favourite Lohrey… One can't help but think of *We Need to Talk about Kevin*… but this is far more subtle and intimate.' Jaclyn Crupi

'In this fine, sensory work Amanda Lohrey spirals imagination, ideas and humanity into a refuge.' Joy Lawn

'Fascinating…Written in meticulously crafted prose, *The Labyrinth* is a deeply satisfying work of fiction which repays close reading and would be a wonderful choice for book groups that enjoy the literature of ideas.' Lisa Hill

'Haunting…A meditation on fundamental patterns in nature and in familial relations…[with a] narrative so bracing—like salt spray stinging your face—that one is borne forward inexorably… Taut, deftly edited…The novel's story is stark, unflinching— gothic without contrivance…Summary does scant justice to the subtlety and power of Lohrey's writing…Every page of this densely populated novel, with its incised landscape, shimmers.' Morag Fraser, *Australian Book Review*

'My novel of the year, full stop…A story told without a syllable of excess sentiment or false feeling, yet which sails full square into the mystic.' Geordie Williamson, *Australian*

'Iridescent…*The Labyrinth* is a nuanced and engrossing novel of bread and bones broken, the trace and rack of violence, and threads that lead the way out of exile.' Felicity Plunkett, *Saturday Paper*

'An impressive addition to Lohrey's body of fiction…A short novel of deep wisdom about nature and art, men and women, motherhood and home…Elegant sentences move with the mindful pace of footsteps on a pathway.' Susan Wyndham, *Age*

'A haunting narrative about loss and self-understanding…Lohrey's descriptions are elegant and transfixing…There is something dreamlike about the novel.' Gretchen Shirm, *Australian*

'Lohrey's writing is typically supple and luminous, her spare narrative counterpointed with vivid, detailed, often enigmatic dreams. By the end…the reader [is ready] to go back and relish again at leisure this author's precise and shining prose.' Katharine England, *Advertiser*

'A deeply meditative book…Beautifully layered, rich in imagery and meaning…It is a sharply tuned novel, a sprawling narrative that resists rigid expectations, instead allowing those who inhabit the pages to surrender themselves to the mode of "reversible destiny" that it is constructed around.' Bec Kavanagh, *Guardian*

'Fluid, dreamlike…Beautifully written and compellingly personal…Lohrey delicately describes these characters with an impressive depth.' *Otago Daily Times*

'Lohrey brings all her skill to this compelling and contemplative novel, which will linger in your mind long after you read the final page.' Claire Nichols, ABC RN

'This novel is her very best. It is perfectly balanced and completely masterful.' Chris Gordon, *Readings Monthly*

Amanda Lohrey lives in Tasmania and writes fiction and non-fiction. She has taught at the University of Tasmania, the University of Technology Sydney and the University of Queensland. Amanda is a regular contributor to the *Monthly* magazine and a former senior fellow of the Australia Council's Literature Board. She received the 2012 Patrick White Award. *The Labyrinth* (2021), her eighth work of fiction, won the Miles Franklin Literary Award, a Prime Minister's Literary Award, a Tasmanian Literary Award and the Voss Literary Prize.

The Labyrinth

A PASTORAL

Amanda Lohrey

TEXT PUBLISHING MELBOURNE AUSTRALIA

The Text Publishing Company acknowledges the Traditional Owners of the country on which we work, the Wurundjeri people of the Kulin Nation, and pays respect to their Elders past and present.

textpublishing.com.au

The Text Publishing Company
Wurundjeri Country, Level 6, Royal Bank Chambers, 287 Collins Street, Melbourne, Victoria 3000 Australia

First published by The Text Publishing Company, 2020
This edition published 2023
Reprinted 2024

Cover image & design by W. H. Chong
Page design by Jessica Horrocks
Typeset by J&M Typesetting

Printed and bound in Australia by Griffin Press, an accredited ISO/NZS 14001:2004 Environmental Management System printer.

ISBN: 9781922458469 (paperback)
ISBN: 9781925923544 (ebook)

A catalogue record for this book is available from the National Library of Australia.

The cure for many ills, noted Jung, is to build something.

Part 1

**what comes after
the father**

Let me begin in my father's house.

I grew up in an asylum, a manicured madhouse. The lawns were kept trim and the flowerbeds in bloom all year round. My father Kenneth Marsden was the chief medical officer, meaning he was a psychiatrist, and unlike his colleagues who were happy to escape the institution as soon as their roster hours had expired, Ken chose to live within the compound. I say compound but in fact Melton Park was more like a country estate, with grand Victorian edifices, barrack-like courtyards, a tall clock tower and banks of exotic flowers. And bulbs in spring that bloomed beneath massive oak and sycamore trees that offered shade from the punishing sun, not for the inmates but for the nurses who sat under them on short breaks, smoking and gossiping. There was of course a security system but it was concealed to the outside observer. There were no bars on windows, though a dry moat ran around a certain high-walled enclosure.

Today I am returning for the first time. The sky is

a washed-out blue and the narrow road in is flanked on either side by bleached pastureland, the grass faded to straw, the sheep clustering under a Lebanese cedar. The great iron gates of the asylum stand permanently open, for the asylum is decommissioned and popular with visitors in search of antique horror. A minibus loaded with Chinese tourists cruises past and I follow it down the long avenue of silky oaks towards the grand clock tower. How abject it looks now, its sandstone face crumbling at the edges, the big round face with the hands stopped at a quarter to nine.

I park beside an abandoned building, its windows broken, its tin guttering left to sag and flap in the breeze. After a long drive I am hungry, and I look for the asylum church that has been converted into a café. Its rustic timber cladding is weathered but the roof looks new, its eaves and finials freshly painted white.

This is the place where I knew my mother, knew her for the first and last time.

Behind the church, next to a pair of dilapidated tennis courts is a sandstone cottage, its windows boarded up with rough wooden planks. Here I lived with my father and my younger brother, Axel, until I was nineteen. My mother, Irene, ran away the week before my tenth birthday. When I found the courage to ask my father why she hadn't taken me with her, Ken seemed unperturbed. 'She was in a hurry,' he said. 'She will be back.'

He was wrong. Not long before Irene disappeared

I had overheard a heated exchange between my parents in which my mother expressed her unease at the recent admission of a man who had murdered his wife and chopped her up in a blender. He was a botanist (said to be a genius) and had asked for a small plot of land in the security zone where he could grow flowers. Ken had authorised the purchase of seeds.

In that first year of my mother's absence there were many nights when I could hear Axel sobbing, hear him through the attic bedroom wall that separated us. If the crying persisted I would climb into his bed, and he would turn his back to me and we would nestle together like spoons, and I would smell his boy smell and lie with him until we both fell asleep.

The inside of the church is humid. Flies buzz around the door and are shooed away by a young waitress in a black singlet, tight black shorts and red Doc Martens. I order from the blackboard and carry my plastic number-on-a-stick to the outdoor tables, where a band of ageing musicians is setting up under a canvas awning. It's all so familiar. The small meeting room at the back of the church, now the café kitchen, is where my brother and I had attended Sunday school with the Reverend James Harwood, a lumbering giant of a man in whose meaty fingers the Bible looked like a fragile thing. The Reverend was near-sighted to the point of blindness, and the lenses of his spectacles so thick that they magnified the pupils of his eyes into two milky orbs, like marbles. All through the Bible lesson he would squint over our heads at the light coming in through the small Gothic window above the door. Jesus is hungry but the fig tree has leaves and no fruit. The Messiah is enraged and curses the tree so that it withers. 'This is the one time that Jesus performs a miracle devoid of mercy, and he did this my dear ones to confound our expectations, to show us that He knows more than we do. Remember that, children, when you are tempted by Satan into doubt. It's a mistake ever to try to second-guess the Lord.'

I remember this because I had never heard the term 'second-guess' and had to ask my father what it meant. But Ken had laughed, and said: 'I wouldn't worry about that.' I asked him once about God the Father and why we had to have two fathers, one invisible. Again he laughed, and said he would explain when I was older.

The four musos are warming up. They are lean and worn-looking, as if somewhere in the past they have been used and discarded. The singer, a woman in her fifties, is haggard, her lank greying hair tied back in a spiky knot. The guitar player strums a rhythmic intro; she taps her right foot three times and opens her mouth. And oh, that voice: that voice is a revelation. It's as if she is channelling Billie Holiday, so smooth, so assured is her soft crooning.

In my childhood there had been music here. On Friday afternoons there would be a tea dance in the church hall. A jazz band made up of staff and inmates would play, and staff and inmates would dance together. Every Friday of the year without fail, except Good Friday, and once when there was an outbreak of dysentery. My father played the clarinet in the asylum jazz combo, and after school Axel and I would stand behind a white-clothed trestle table and snigger at the monotonous foxtrot shuffle of the dancers, their jolting jitterbug, their hectic arm-pumping swirls in the final waltz that would signal it was time to lay out the sandwiches and scones.

I leave the café garden and walk towards the Italianate portal of what was once the nurses' quarters, now a collection of vintage shops. On either side of a long central hallway there are small rooms like monks' cells, bedrooms for the nurses with high ceilings that were cool in the hot summers: intimate spaces, each with its narrow iron-frame bed, its modest wooden chest of drawers, its small swivel mirror. Now they are crammed with dusty books and furniture, dun-coloured stoneware jars, Victorian ruby glassware, vintage leather coats, and antique dolls with rouged ceramic cheeks and glass eyes that stare out into space with a petrified gaze.

One of my father's reforms had been to set up a workshop, along with a craft studio. This was a source of pride to him, for he believed in the mind as a divine engineering project designed for the invention and use of tools. *Homo faber*: man the maker. The use of the hands is a powerful medicine, he would say. We can succumb to the temptation to overthink a problem when the cure for many ills is to make something. This was one of his favourite maxims and he repeated it often, and on one occasion cited Jung (though he otherwise thought him a charlatan). It was Ken's own experience that counted, for growing up on a small dairy farm had instilled in him a certain practicality, a childhood of rising in the dark to milk cows and school holidays spent mending fences. A man who does not use his hands is a mind untethered, he would say: when you make something you become a rivet in the fabric of the real. On his way home from the wards he would drop by the asylum workshop to inspect the pottery, the water-colours, the basketwork and rug-making. Nothing gave him greater pleasure, but in this as in other matters he did not regard himself as progressive—did not object, for example, to the term lunatic. We are all affected by the moon, he would say, just some of us more than others.

At the rear of the family cottage he had built his own workshop where, after Irene disappeared, he made me a doll's house with a circular staircase that I could never gaze on without a sense of the mystery of my own being. I would imagine that somewhere in the attic of the doll's house, my mother had left behind a part of herself and that one day she would return for it.

The only other woman in the family was Ken's sister, Ruth. Ruth had trained as a nurse in a bush hospital and shipped to London in her twenties. For many years all we knew of her was that she lived somewhere in a place called Essex with a much older husband and no children. On birthdays and at Christmas she sent us presents—a book on the Tower of London, a jigsaw of the British Isles—never anything that interested us. But one day there arrived a foldout set of postcards of Ely Cathedral, and it was one of these that struck me with an uncanny familiarity verging on awe. It was an image of the cathedral's Lady Chapel, its walls lined with rows of statues. But the startling thing was this: the larger statues had been hacked from their niches and the faces of the smaller figures mutilated with hammers, their eyes gouged out, their features obliterated. 'Over one hundred and forty of them,' Ruth had written, 'most, it is thought, of the Virgin Mother.'

'Fanatics,' Ken had pronounced over supper, and he explained to me and to Axel the Protestant hatred of images. After supper he had put the postcards in the cupboard of the sideboard and when he had gone to bed I opened the cupboard, tore out the image of the Lady Chapel and took it up to my room, where I hid it in a drawer beneath my underwear. From time to time I would take it out and gaze at it with furtive fascination. It was as if I had dreamed it: the smashed faces of the saints. Like my mother: there and not there.

Axel and I were allowed to roam the asylum freely and often I sought out the company of the young nurses, who gave me sweets and felt sorry for me because my mother had bolted. Later, in the long summer before university I worked in the big kitchen, averting my eyes from the slimy porridge, the fat pink saveloys, the grey mincemeat in watery gravy. Ken decided then that I should assist at some sessions of shock treatment. 'People will tell you harsh things about this, Erica, because they haven't seen it work.' But on the two occasions that I attended as an observer I threw up, after which he excused me from any further involvement. I did not, he said, have the stomach for medicine.

In the end it was Axel who was press-ganged into a medical degree while I spent two years studying Latin and Greek. My schoolgirl Latin, coached by my father, had been good, and the university had offered Greek for beginners. Soon it became clear that I had an aptitude, a gift for entering wholly into another world, whether Melton Park or the gods on Olympus it made no difference. And Ken had encouraged me. For as long as I could remember he had exhibited a wry fondness for Latin mottoes, and one in particular. When a diagnosis had been proved wrong, a prescribed treatment had failed, or some other unforeseen event had transpired, occasionally he would discuss it with Axel and me over dinner, and would pronounce: *Dis aliter visum.* Which we soon came to know meant: The gods thought otherwise. So it was that as a student I lost myself in the most arcane and useless study I could find, until the gods thought otherwise and I abandoned my studies to run off with the artist Gabriel Priest. But by then my father was dead.

It's almost four in the afternoon and I have walked over most of the estate but still I haven't found it: the labyrinth. How could I have forgotten its location? I was sure that it sat in the courtyard behind the clock tower, a pattern of red-brick and terracotta paving. But when I look there is only a patchy lawn of dry, uneven grass. Here in the evenings Axel and I had played by our own rules, each rule designed to hinder the other from reaching the centre; variations on hopscotch to begin with that became more and more arbitrary, wilful and competitive: no crossing the lines, and remembering passwords conjured at short notice that had to be shouted whenever we passed one another on the path. The pattern of the labyrinth was meaningless but it fascinated us both, for it seemed to suggest the possibility of another reality, a mystical geometry of secret formulae and magic spells, of alchemy in brick and a mathematical wizardry that Axel explored more conscientiously than I. He was a shy boy, anxious to please, and I would sometimes catch my father watching him: perplexed and wary, he would encourage Axel with a tender concern that could make me jealous. Some summer evenings after work, Ken would walk the labyrinth with us, would produce a tape measure from his pocket and demand that we estimate the co-ordinates of a section, nominated by him, which would then be measured out by Axel while I made little attempt to hide my boredom. I was not compliant; I withdrew into the gap where my mother had been. It was typical of Ken that he never told us the story of the Minotaur. For Ken it was all about the co-ordinates. Evil was a chemical malfunction in the brain.

By late afternoon there is only one place left to look, and I walk up the hill to a squat building in the style of Victorian gothic that had once been the women's ward and is now another antique shop of musty alcoves crammed with old books and furniture. It's an octagonal building in which the beds, separated by partitions, faced a central station where the nurses had desks and the inmates' cubicles radiated out like canisters on a flywheel. As a child I would hover around the nurses' station, fascinated by the high shelves of medication, brown glass bottles of pills locked behind the doors of a cedar cupboard. A tall, sombre woman named Grace, a mute, had taken a shine to me; whenever I entered the ward she would appear and follow close behind, solemn and intent. 'Don't worry about Grace,' one of the jolly young nurses had said, 'she's decided it's her job to protect you from the others.' Soon I got used to this phantom guardian and would sometimes try to bamboozle her by darting behind doors or crouching under beds while Grace stood bewildered in the aisle, rigid as a statue.

Behind a large circular desk a woman is sitting beside an old-fashioned cash register and playing Solitaire on her iPad. She looks up grudgingly when interrupted. Does she by any chance know what happened to the labyrinth? The woman shrugs. 'Neil who runs the café grew up around here,' she says. 'Ask him.'

In the café, Neil is packing up for the day. He is a heavy-set man in his forties who does not look me in the eye. 'The labyrinth? They dug it out. It was all overgrown and good for nothing.'

'I used to play on it as a child.'

'Yeah? Well, it had some lovely colonial bricks, the orange ones, handmade by convicts. They've stacked them up in the old bakery.' He moves across to the entrance, where he lowers the blind on the door with a sudden snap.

'Do you know if they're for sale?'

'They were, but they're not now. I put in a bid for 'em. Got 'em cheap.'

'I suppose you could use them for paving.'

'Don't need any paving.' The dishcloth hangs limply in his hand. 'They'll make a nice pizza oven.'

That night, at my roadside motel, I sleep soundly, drifting off with the image of the clock tower in my mind's eye. This was my unlikely beginning: in the midst of madness I had been happy. It was a place of great suffering, people said, and former inmates come forward on television, still, after all these years, to weep over their incarceration in Melton Park. But Axel and I had roamed the place with perfect freedom. Our father indulged us, and our mother's absence gave me licence to do as I pleased. Ken had one day confessed that in giving his children this freedom he had perhaps overcompensated for Irene's flight, though he had watched us closely for signs of mourning. Some weeks after Irene disappeared he gave me a set of small stuffed animals and instructed me to play with them on the floor of his office for an hour, once a week, while he sat and observed me.

When I was old enough to be curious I asked him about these sessions and he said he would show me his notes from that time, when I turned twenty-one. But he died a week before my twentieth birthday. A patient attacked him with a scythe that had been left lying in the garden and severed his carotid artery. Before he could be found he had bled to death on a bank of pink azaleas.

Since then I have had a recurring dream. My father is sitting under one of the sycamore trees near the entrance to the asylum church. He is wearing a broad-brimmed straw hat, such as he never owned, and he is playing his clarinet. I am loitering behind a tree and straining to hear the music. Is it Mozart? Or some jazz improvisation in the Benny Goodman style that he loved? The notes glide on the air, pure and true, but there is interference coming from the clock tower that strikes the hour; again the notes swoop and dive, then fade, then build once more, at first warm and mellow, then bright and clear. But the clock tower goes on striking the hour, though the hour has not yet arrived: striking over and over, so that I am unable to make out the melody.

o

My son's first trial lasted for twenty-eight days. The jury could not agree on a verdict and was dismissed, the agony prolonged. The second jury was conclusive.

A week after Daniel was sentenced I studied a map of the Napier Valley, where the new private prison sits in the heart of sheep-grazing country: metal and concrete and barbed wire on a pasture of shrivelled grass.

The town nearest to the prison is Brockwood, which lies not in the valley but on the coast. Behind Brockwood is a low mountain range and on the inland side of the mountains is the Napier Valley, an old coal-mining precinct. From here the coast can only be accessed by a narrow pass of thirty-six hairpin bends: built by convicts in the 1840s and densely forested on either side it winds in a meandering descent to the coast, so that at each bend there is a glimpse of the ocean that extends like a mirage to the horizon.

In Brockwood I spend my first night in a cheap motel room under thin blankets of faded cream wool, their satin trim fraying at the edges. In the morning, at a café on the esplanade I eat breakfast, seated behind a row of life-size fibreglass dolphins frozen in mid-frolic. There is a pale wintry sun. The esplanade is crowded with visitors and has the smell of seaside towns everywhere: salt, fish-and-chip fat, burnt coffee and oily sunscreen. Seagulls perch on the bollards of the marina, alert and quarrelsome. Outside the Thai restaurant a young man in shorts and thongs is leaning against the wall, hungover, or perhaps stoned. The hair on his bare legs has a golden sheen and his ragged blond hair, stiff with salt, frames his slack features. In one hand he clutches an oily white paper bag of hot food while with the other he attempts clumsily to manipulate his phone, managing twice to drop it with a snapping sound onto the bitumen. Large fat chips spill from the bag across the pavement as he bends unsteadily to retrieve the phone. Mission accomplished he leans back against the wall, eyes glazed and unfocussed, body splayed as if the effort of it has unhinged all his joints. From across the road a Pacific gull has been watching him. It begins to wend its way through the double lane of cruising traffic, hopping in the narrow spaces between the cars, its timing uncanny, its beak pointed with loaded intent, and I cannot take my eyes off it, for it has all the clarity of will and focus that the young man lacks. With one final hop it pounces on the scattered chips at his feet, just as he extends a grubby-thonged foot to kick in its direction, feebly, and again almost falls headlong into the gutter. 'Fuck off!' he hisses, righting himself against the wall with one arm. The phone now safely in his pocket, he buries his face in the greasy paper bag to bite into whatever is left. The seagull mean-while has scavenged the last chip on the pavement and is hopping insouciantly back across the road towards the safety of the sea wall.

No. Not Brockwood. This is not the place.

I return to my car and head north. Here the freeway runs close beside the coast, so close that at high tide the foamy wash of the surf is only metres from the edge of the bitumen. Forty minutes beyond Brockwood I reach a turn-off and the sign *Garra Nalla 5 km*. I look across the dry sheep paddocks between the freeway and the ocean and can see a small settlement set on a grassy headland some thirty metres or so above sea level.

The road in runs alongside reedy marshland, a breeding ground for black swans that congregate on the brackish water. It terminates beside a deep lagoon where the outgoing tide is flowing into the ocean and a row of pied cormorants are standing to attention on an exposed sandbank like a line of sentries. I turn away from the water and drive up a steep hill towards a cluster of houses that sit atop the spectacular headland, and from there I cruise slowly along the network of narrow unsealed roads that crisscross the settlement. There must be a hundred or so dwellings here, some with lush gardens, others bare and with the aura of rarely visited shacks. There is no shop, no pub, no petrol bowser. Nothing.

I glance at my watch: almost noon. Down the hill then to the terminus of the main road, and the turning circle beside the lagoon where I park next to the picnic table and take out my laptop to look at rentals. There is one, a fibro shack on a flat area behind the sand dunes. Rough and bare, it is likely to be within my means. I ring the agent.

A young man arrives in a white ute with a surfboard strapped to the roof of the cabin. He introduces himself as Job and when he hands me his card I see that he spells it Jobe, as if adding an 'e' will protect him from the unhappy fate of the original. He is eager to tell me that as a matter of fact he lives in Garra Nalla himself and it's a great place, very private, if that's what I am looking for and I say, yes, that is exactly what I am looking for. Jobe is just a kid, no more than twenty-five with bleached hair and a thin tie, the knot of which sits halfway down his shirt in a larrikin noose so that I wonder why he bothers. I follow him along a flat sandy drive behind the dunes until we come to the single-storey shack, grey, weathered and unkempt. Jobe pauses on the threshold, a concrete terrace, derelict and with tufts of grass sprouting through the cracks. 'A bit of Roundup'll fix that,' he says. 'Have to be honest with you. The owner has neglected the place.' He wrenches the key in the lock, which sticks. 'That's why it's cheap.'

Inside, the air smells of dust. Jobe sneezes. 'Built in the nineteen-twenties,' he sniffs. 'Bigger than it looks.' Which it is, a jumble of rooms that appear to have been added in different eras and connected by short passageways as if the house is an organic puzzle that has evolved without planning. Unlike most fibro shacks it has a pitched roof and wide overhanging eaves that will keep it cool in summer. The living room is lined with dark-stained dado board and there is a red-brick fireplace and an old-fashioned picture rail around the walls. The kitchen is surprisingly large, with an old wood stove in cast iron and a tin flue reaching up through the plasterboard ceiling. The casement windows are cedar and the floor is pitted cork, bleached by the sun. When I stand in the middle of the room I see that it is exactly square and perfectly proportioned; all the fittings are in the right place and sit well together, so that it feels like a room with a living centre.

'Who owns this place?' I ask.

'Some cranky old coot. Never met him.'

I observe how the hallway is lined with handsome doors rescued from at least one older building and there is not a single cheap plywood door of the kind that has a hollow core. Instead the doors are pine and oak, no doubt salvaged from demolition sites, and while each has its own character this lack of uniformity is not chaotic but creates an effect of liveliness. The house breathes.

The main bedroom is spacious, with a scuffed oak floor and another bay window that looks out to the hills. But the two small bedrooms are pokey and lined with brown unpainted Masonite, and one of them has been covered in pages from old colour magazines in an effect of faded decoupage. In all the rooms the venetian blinds are dusty and flyblown, but intact.

We return to the kitchen, where Jobe unlocks the back door and we step outside. Above the window of the north-facing bedroom a cone-shaped nest of compacted mud is tucked in under the eaves. Small grey feathers snag in the flyscreen and grey-white bird shit is splattered on the narrow concrete path that winds around the house.

'Swallows,' says Jobe. 'Supposed to be lucky.' His eagerness to please is touching. I remark on how the rear of the house is almost against its western fence, a ragged line of wooden posts and sagging barbed wire, leaving a wide bare space on the eastern side between the house and the dunes.

'Yeah, funny the way they've built it, all over on the one side.' He stares at the dry sandy flat, a stretch of stunted grass and the sickly yellow of flowering capeweed. 'You could put a cricket pitch in there.'

'Indeed, you could,' I say, though a cricket pitch is not what I have in mind. We agree that I will follow Jobe back to Brockwood and sign a lease, but already I have decided I will buy this house. Later, I persuade Jobe to give me the owner's number—'probably shouldn't do this'—and that night I ring him.

He is an old man with an old man's voice, high and dry and whiny. He complains about the upkeep of the place and the rates, and that no one in the family ever wants to go there.

'Well, sell it to me.'

There is a long pause. 'I'll think about it.' And then: 'What did you say your name was, missus?'

'Marsden. Erica Marsden.'

'Haven't I heard that name somewhere before?

'I don't know. Have you?'

Someone is going to recognise me, even here.

°

It's just after three in the afternoon and the removalists stomp about the shack in their boots, two brawny young men in a sweat. In the living room a blue-tongue lizard waddles onto the warm stone hearth and one of them pulls up short, backing his mate into a wall.

'Fuck, a snake!'

'Geez, you're an idiot. It's a goanna.'

'An easy mistake to make,' I say, glad they have been the first to see its vestigial legs, so comically out of proportion to the thickness of its body. The two men stare for a moment as the blue-tongue scampers across the hearth and into a low hole in the fibro wall beside the fireplace. The older of the two nods at the hole in the wall. 'Needs some spackle there,' he says. 'You'll be doing some repairs to this place, I reckon.'

By four in the afternoon they are gone. Packing boxes are stacked against the walls along with furniture covered in grey serge blankets. The house was sold to me as empty but in the largest of the bedrooms a big old-fashioned wardrobe has been left behind, a three-door unit in shiny dark walnut with a curved door at the centre that opens onto a column of cedar drawers. In the coming days I will arrange for it to be removed. Although handsome, it reeks of a stale intimacy.

I take some linen from the car, make up a bed and unpack a small suitcase of clothes. In the chaos of the living room a mellow light is slanting through the half-drawn blinds and pooling on the bare floorboards. The sun is low over the distant hills and I can hear the rustle of swallows under the eaves. I climb onto a chair to hang one of my son's paintings from the dark-stained picture rail; it's the only one of his works left since he burned his canvases: a self-portrait in charcoal with a vivid red slash of paint across the forehead. For a long time I couldn't bring myself to hang it, but now in the artless jumble of this shack it looks as if it belongs.

Weary, I make myself a sandwich and some tea. In an hour I will go to bed early and lie propped up on two pillows so that I can see the moon through the window.

I have arrived. I have found the place.

○

Two weeks on, and I stand at the open door and listen to the roar of the sea coming from beyond the dunes. Am I at home in this place? Not yet, but I had better get used to it. The house is gritty with sand that blows in through the wire screens, dead flies appear where I have swept just the day before and I need to install an iron lid for the chimney. The sunroom and two of the bedrooms are crammed with boxes still unpacked.

At eight in the morning I light the cast-iron stove which I have learned to operate from a faded sheet of instructions that a former tenant has left Blu-Tacked to the wall, the same tenant who presumably left the wood and the number of Joe the wood carter, whom I am about to ring. I walk to the sink and half-fill a glass with luke-warm water from the tap. The corrugated-iron tank is old and rusted, and I have ordered two new tanks in dark green plastic, one for me and one for the fire service since this is an area prone to bushfire. Just four years ago a fire swept through the settlement with little warning and the residents had to stand chest-deep in the lagoon until rescued by boats. And soon I must attend to the roof and the guttering. The birds and the possums shit on the roof and I am probably drinking E. coli.

My days have no routine. I do things impulsively, waiting for the day when I can visit Daniel in the new prison. This morning when I got out of bed I began to unpack one of the boxes labelled BOOKS that are stacked in the sunroom. So many books, some in cartons secured with masking tape, some in plastic storage boxes with fitted lids, others in wooden crates. My son was not merely a reader but a collector and now the two smaller bedrooms and the sunroom, an enclosed veranda, are stacked to the ceiling with hundreds of volumes of bound paper destined for incineration (and there are dozens of other cartons that for the moment I have had to put into storage). I can burn only one a day, for I have learned that paper is bad for the wood stove and ash from a paper burn clogs the flue, and even at this rate it will take me years. When Ken died his books were locked away in storage by my brother, who didn't want them but, still in awe of his father, couldn't bring himself to dispose of them. Later he had offered them to Daniel, who had rifled through the boxes with the unselfconscious delight of Aladdin looting a cave. 'Some crazy shit here,' he'd said, while Axel looked on with an expression of disapproval as if to say: He's just like you, reckless and impatient.

I take one of these books to the table now to read while I drink my coffee. When I open it at random my eye goes immediately to the sentence *There is absolutely no problem.* Methodically I tear the pages from the spine and begin to feed them into the stove. One book a day until I have burned the lot. These are my son's instructions: *Burn my books.* Why, Daniel? *They have deceived me.* This was the last coherent thing he said to me before they led him away.

○

Thursday morning. Early. I climb out of bed and shiver in the still-dark house. There is no question of breakfast, for I am too agitated to eat. Instead I linger for a long time in the shower, a narrow enclosure built of prefab fibreglass. Then I stand at the open cupboard where I hang my clothes, unable to decide what to wear. And silently berate myself: This is absurd, I say out loud. I am not a young woman on a date. But I do not want to provoke or upset him.

It's just after eight when I set out and turn off onto the road that runs through the grazing lands that surround Garra Nalla. To my right are sheep paddocks that slope down towards the marshlands, to my left the bare chocolate soil where a young man on a tractor is ploughing furrows for what I guess is a potato crop. Jobe had described the surrounding farmland as 'spud country'. Sheep and spuds, he had said, 'that's what they do here.'

Soon I am at the foot of the narrow mountain pass with its thirty-six hairpin bends that will take me up and into the Napier Valley. The pass is surrounded on all sides by dry sclerophyll forest scarred by a recent bushfire, so that pale feathery shoots of epicormic growth sprout from blackened trunks. At the top is the little town of Mt Godwin, a row of weathered veranda shopfronts miraculously spared by the flames.

It's a bright morning, crisp and dry, and the paddocks and hedges of the valley are covered in an unseasonal white frost. This valley is a cold place, a string of towns that were supposed to grow and prosper, but in the 1970s a deep seam of coal caught alight and the main mine had to be abandoned (if I turn my head and look to the hills I can see a thin waft of smoke rising through the trees). Now the valley is sparsely populated, except for the new prison that sits among the paddocks, hard-edged and shiny, a complex of massive silver boxes deposited by aliens.

The gaol is said to be a model of its kind but my son is in maximum security and has no privileges. As I drive along the final straight beside frostbitten fields I begin to see flashes of his face in the windscreen and I am unnerved; my gut spasms and I pull over to the side of the road, fling open the car door and scramble down a steep bank to vomit into a hawthorn bush.

A car slows behind me and a young man in a high-vis vest sticks his head out the driver's window. 'You okay, lady?'

I raise my head to him, dizzy and unseeing, beyond shame. My hair snags on a low-lying branch laden with the last of its red winter berries and my fingers prick on the sharp thorns.

'Fine. Thanks.' I can barely speak for heaving. I stagger up the bank, picking at sticky strands of hair that cling to my mouth, and give a weak nod in the direction of the stranger. Back in my car I sit in a cold sweat and stare ahead, waiting for my good Samaritan to cruise on out of sight.

The metallic walls of the prison glint above the frost-covered fields. Along the denuded mining ridge of the hills the wind turbines stand like elegant guards, their blades becalmed in the harsh light. In the parking lot I follow the instructions from Jodie, my contact from the prisoners' support group. Jodie's husband, a drug dealer, is in for manslaughter and seems to be some kind of prison warlord, privy to the goings-on in the gaol and prepared to give out information if Jodie approves of the enquirer. I have met Jodie only once, in a coffee shop in the city, and she must have decided I could be trusted because she has been forthcoming ever since.

I leave my phone and handbag in the car, walk to the gates and press the button. 'They'll leave you hanging,' Jodie had said. 'They look at you from inside on a camera, so pretend you're not bothered.' I try to appear casual, and gaze around me as if admiring the scenery: the dome-shaped hill to the south, the tangle of willow trees along the narrow riverbed, the white cockatoos foraging by the road.

The electronic gate slides open.

Inside, I am directed across a yard to a checkpoint. A short middle-aged woman with a baby face and a peroxided pony-tail asks to see my driver's licence.

'You're here for the prisoner Daniel Priest. That correct?'

I nod. The warder pats me down and points to the guillotine frame of a metal detector. From there I am ushered to an X-ray machine where my guts are illuminated and I feel for an instant as if my bones might melt into a viscous glue.

The walls of the visitors' room are a violent mustard yellow. On one wall there is a huge mural of crudely drawn trees and boulders in shades of muddy orange and greenish brown. It has the quality of sludge. Two warders escort me to a steel table, bolted to the floor, and I sit on a steel chair, also bolted to the floor. Everything here is steel and concrete; even the air has a metallic taste. And the room is so very empty, for I am visiting by special arrangement; there will be no other prisoners and no other visitors.

The door clangs open and my son, in an orange boilersuit, is shuffling towards me in shackles. He is so volatile, his rages so great that he must be visited alone as his ranting disturbs other families. I have been warned: if the rages persist, all visitation rights will be cancelled.

Daniel slumps into the chair opposite me and I see that he is weeping. The shock of this almost undoes me. I feared that I might be the one to cry. He has a large bruise on his left cheek and his fine-boned hands are red raw. He wipes his eyes with chafed fingers and stares ahead at the mural on the wall. 'Rubbish,' he mumbles, shaking his head. Then he looks up to the ceiling and roars: 'Rubbish!'

One of the warders looks across. He is alert, ready to move. I glance at him and shake my head. 'It's okay,' I mouth.

'Yes, it's horrible,' I say. 'Who could paint anything so ugly?'

Daniel leans back in his steel chair and closes his eyes, as if the sight of it is too much of an affront to bear.

Here we are, then, framed by this ghastly mural with its thickly drawn lines, its muddy palette, its jagged rocks. I know better than to react, for I know what is happening here. My son is an artist; he has done nothing in his adult life but daub canvas, nothing, that is, until his crime. Like any fantasist he believed he could remake the world in his own image, and when that failed he had no alternative but to smash it up: the world, that is. His, and mine.

Back home, I drop my keys onto the kitchen table and collapse into a chair. The afternoon darkens. The sun sets over the hills. The moon comes out. But still my body won't move. I must get up, I think, I must get out of this chair. My mouth is dry. I must drink something. I am cold. There is a rug on the couch opposite and I could reach out for it. I could reach out for the rug but my arms are lead. It's as if my body has unlearned everything it knew.

o

The weather turns and is suddenly warm. At the weekend, families come and settle in at the beach with their children, their bright towels, their trail bikes, their lobster sunburn.

My nearest neighbours are Lynnie and Ray Gittus,

a couple in late middle age who live in an old settler's cottage set back from the road. With its rose bushes and neatly mowed lawn it looks suburban; there is a white picket fence, freshly painted, and on either side of its little gate stand two tin statues of pink flamingos, their feathers weathered into a greyish ochre.

On my walks I often pass by Lynnie, who looks after the grounds of several of the shack owners. Clad in a black leather bikie's jacket with a skull and crossbones on the back, her head encased in goggles and industrial earmuffs, she looks formidable, manoeuvring her noisy ride-on mower like a veteran aviatrix, temporarily grounded. Whenever she sees me she is in the habit of giving a thumbs up, but one morning she had cut the engine, pulled off the goggles and beckoned me from across the road. 'Don't be a stranger,' she said. 'Come in for a coffee.'

'That would be nice.'

'Tomorrow morning suit you?'

Without her armour, Lynnie is a wiry woman with reddish curls and pale freckled skin. She wears no makeup other than to pencil her eyebrows into thin black arcs.

I walk up the steps of the veranda where Ray Gittus is slumped in a battered cane chair, propped up by pillows. He is a heavily built man run to seed, with shoulders of compacted muscle and wasted calves that seem to dangle from his khaki shorts so that his feet barely touch the ground. His thinning black hair is greying and his skin is sallow. Beside him on a small wicker table is an alarm clock of the old-fashioned kind, the size of a bread and butter plate, with two chrome bells on top and a small chrome hammer that activates the alarm. He sees me staring at it and I look away.

Lynnie beckons me into the kitchen where she is pouring water from the kettle into a large brown teapot. 'Ray's not himself,' she says.

'He's unwell?'

'Had to retire early. Worked for years as a roustabout for the Napiers.'

The Napiers are the local squatters, sheep graziers with a vast swathe of land in the valley that bears their name.

'He must miss it.'

'He doesn't miss the turbines.'

'The turbines?'

'You know, the wind turbines. All along the old mining ridges there, dozens and dozens of 'em. They make that *whup whup* noise. They call it infrasound. Heard of that?'

'Yes.'

'Thank God we moved here. The turbines drove Ray mad. He was all right until they put those things in. Now he has his torments.'

'Really? What are his...' I hesitate. 'What are his symptoms?'

'It's his legs. They ache. It's painful for him to walk.' She lowers her voice. 'Something in his mind's not right.

He broods on things. Dinny, up the road,' she nods in the direction of the turn-off, 'said he could get him some marijuana for it but Ray won't hear of it. He's always been teetotal. Kind of Dinny to offer, though.'

'Who's Dinny?'

'Dinny works for the council in weed control.' Lynnie grins, winking at me, then looks anxiously over her shoulder in the direction of the veranda. 'The gorse is taking over,' she says, in a loud voice. 'That and the Spanish heath.' She lowers her voice again. 'Now that Ray can't work anymore he won't leave the house, except to see the doc. Just sits on the veranda and stares into space, poor old bugger. You wouldn't think it but he was an active man once, captain of the volunteer fire service in these parts.'

'There was a big fire here, wasn't there?'

'Oh, yes, big all right.' She starts, and looks out to the veranda. The alarm on the clock beside Ray is emitting a shrill tinny alert. 'He's done it again,' she mutters and heads for the door.

I drain my mug, certain that I should leave Lynnie to deal with the alarm. I pause on the threshold of the veranda, where Ray glowers at me like a sullen child.

Lynnie follows me out and down the path to stand at the gate, flanked by the tin flamingos and with her arms folded across her apron. 'Well, thanks for coming.'

I nod in the direction of the veranda. 'What's with the alarm clock?'

Lynnie sighs and shakes her head. 'You wouldn't believe me if I told you.'

Late afternoon, I step out into the garden to water a row of river wattles I have planted along the fence line. I am dribbling water from the hose onto the delicate fronds of their lacy foliage when I see a small snake lying half under the wire fence, a young copperhead less than a metre long. The hose jerks in my hand so that water sprays onto my feet but I recover, for I see that the snake is distressed and appears to be caught in the fence. I walk toward it until I am close enough to see that it's limp, half-dead. I drop the hose and pick up a rake that sits against the fence, and poke at the snake with the end of the long handle to see if I can release it, but the snake twitches and goes limp again. I walk across to the shack where a spade is propped beside the back door and hope that by the time I return the snake will have freed itself and slithered under the fence to the vacant block of ferns between me and the Gittuses. But when I return it's still there, twitching beneath the wire. Holding my breath I drive the spade into its spine.

The phone is ringing from inside and I leave the hose to dribble in the sand. The tin roof has turned dark against a fiery evening sky. Smoke from a forestry burn-off has created a lurid sunset; great nimbus clouds of burnt coral streak above the horizon and the sun flares low over the hills.

I open the phone and it's my brother. He wants to

know if he can come to visit. 'Not yet, Axel,' I say. 'I'm not ready.'

He begins to remonstrate. 'Erica—'

I hang up. But the timbre of his voice has penetrated my guard; he sounds so much like my father, the same deep, slightly hoarse tone. It's as if a gong has been struck and the vibration continues to resonate in my body in waves, so that I must lie my head on the cool surface of the kitchen table until they have subsided.

o

Why am I here, here behind the dunes in this dusty old shack? To be close to the prison, yes, but there is another reason.

One night, in the city, some months after my son had been sentenced, suddenly I emerged from the limbo that had held me in its suffocating pall. As if waking from a coma into floodlit mania I stood up, rigid, and began to stalk each room of my apartment, looking for something I had mislaid. Something was missing. Where was it? At last, unable to find that thing, I returned to my bed and gulped down a sleeping pill.

When I woke it was from a dream of intense clarity. For a long time I lay on my bed, breathing deeply and bathed in the peculiar light that had irradiated the dream. I was living on a great desert plain, a place of immense horizons and dazzling light where there was no depth of field, no shadow, just a blessed sunlit transparency. In this desert was a city of white walls and low rooftops and at the centre of the city was a vast labyrinth. In an instant I was within the labyrinth but as I approached the centre I woke and sat up in bed with my hands over my eyes, as if to preserve the image of its form, the seductive curves of its sinuous path. But found that I could not recall the pattern, only the sensation of being within it, my myopic focus, and the sight of my feet moving along the sunlit meander, one bare foot after the other. I was too far in, too far in to see the whole of the thing. Too busy looking at my feet.

For days that sensation stayed with me: the immensity of the plain; the freedom from dread; the clarity of the light. The pain of the past months was a hollow sensation in my chest that never went away but in the dream the pain had assumed a shape, something half-apprehended that persisted now like a kernel buried in my brain, a hazy but luminous image projected against the screen of my mind's eye.

I rang an agency and put my apartment on the market. I would go someplace and build this labyrinth: I would make the dream real. First the making—I recalled my father's words: *the cure for many ills is to build something*—and then the repetition, the going over and over so that time would rupture and be stopped in its flow. And I could live in an infinitely expanding present in which there was no nostalgia, no consequence, no outcome or false promise. The future now meant nothing. Since my past and my future were hitched to my son's life sentence, I felt that if I stepped outside the present I risked being turned to stone.

'What will you do with your time there?' Axel had asked when I told him I was moving to the coast. 'If you give up work, you'll just brood all day.' To this there was no answer, or none that would satisfy him. For months I had lived in a fugue state, and knew there was no other cure. And besides, Daniel was soon to be moved to the new prison, a long way from the city. I would go to where this prison was and find the place I needed to be. But Axel was uneasy. You have always been impulsive, he said, chewing at his lip. Until our mother's leaving Axel and I had competed fiercely, often with spite, but with Irene gone we had entered into a silent truce; thereafter the contest seemed pointless. Somewhere in late adolescence it dawned on us that we loved one another. But we had not been comfortable together since he married a woman who judged me, and my son. I could not accept that judgement.

○

It's just after nine in the evening and I open a bottle of wine and carry it into the dusty sunroom, where I have set up a long trestle table and my laptop. The sunroom is a narrow skillion tacked onto the shack as an afterthought, so that its inner wall is the outer wall of the original dwelling and its tin roof is flat and draws the heat. Here I have laid out my papers, mostly designs for labyrinths taken from the internet or photocopied from books.

Now, at night, I pore over dozens of patterns, hundreds if you include the variation in materials. At first I went online to see what I could find but the net is a labyrinth of its own, a flashing series of messages, an echo chamber of disembodied voices that leaves me adrift and unsatisfied. These are the moments when my activity seems preposterous, a deluded attempt at distraction, nutty and futile. I want something to present itself, not as a choice but as a gift. But from where would such a gift come? I shudder now when I recall the first time I visited Daniel after his sentencing. It was in the old prison, now decommissioned, a modified panopticon, a labyrinth of a kind from which all the internal pathways had been removed and all the nodes had been sealed into fixed and frozen spaces.

Beside me is the thick yellow binder where I enter my notes. *The word* labyrinth *comes from the Greek word* labrys, *a double-headed stone axe said to have been a weapon of the Amazons and to symbolise the early forms of matriarchal society. Said also to have been an early symbol of the act of creation, of* techne, *and making by hand.*

I have learned that a simple labyrinth can be laid out by anyone, unlike a maze, which is a puzzle of mostly blind alleys designed for entrapment. The maze is a challenge to the brain (how smart are you), the labyrinth to the heart (will you surrender). In the maze you grapple with the challenge but in the labyrinth you let go. Effortlessly you come back to where you started, somehow changed by the act of surrender. In this way the labyrinth is said to be a model of reversible destiny.

In my notebook I have made a simple drawing of the oldest recorded labyrinth, the so-called seed pattern with its seven pathways, and in my idle moments I am given to doodling this shape, over and over. I like its rounded organic form, its soft asymmetry. There are no straight lines or precise angles: no brittle geometry.

I get up now, out of my chair to stretch, and walk to the kitchen to get some water. There are no lights on, and no moon; the shack is dark but by now it has become an extension of my body; I could find my way around it blindfolded. There are many nights when the glow of my laptop screen is the only light in the house.

Glass in hand I settle again to my notes: my conceptual wallpaper. *The labyrinth is a single path that leads in a convoluted unravelling to its centre, and back out again. Each labyrinth pattern is made up of two essential elements, the meander and the spiral. The meander is the pathway, the groove of time which, while linear, must not be a simple path but intricately coiled so that it doubles back on itself in unexpected turns. As for the spiral, it is the primal image of creation and found just about everywhere, from the double helix of the DNA molecule to the unfolding frond of a fern, to the*

spinning galaxy itself. In the form of the classical labyrinth, or
seed pattern, its opening is said by some to resemble a woman's
labia, its outer rim the cervix, its coils the inner walls of the
womb.

The womb and the labrys axe. Female and male:
mother and father. Except there is no reason why a woman
should not wield an axe.

There is much that I have not bothered to enter in
my yellow binder, some of it esoteric, residues of primitive superstition along with mediaeval theories of sacred
geometry and the power of numbers. None of this speaks
to me, and I am out of sympathy with the more specula-
tive New Age websites with their reach for the sacred.
Were it not for the spell cast by my dream, by the force
and clarity of it, which remains with me still, I would not
persevere. And then there is that flat, sandy expanse of
ground between the shack and the dunes that I think of
as the gap. Dead space, so abject, so derelict, it demands to
be redeemed. I could plant a garden but the conditions are
severe: salt, wind and sand. Nature alone is not enough.
Some artefact, some human hand is demanded.

By now it is almost 2 a.m. and the pattern of my sleep-
lessness persists. Beside my bed is a small white plastic
bottle of sleeping pills but since arriving at Garra Nalla
I have yet to take one. Here in this little hamlet I have
resolved to own the anguish of my nights, and if I am
lethargic during the day then what does it matter? As long
as I am not in a hot flush of panic it's okay not to sleep, and

when my labyrinth is constructed I think I might prefer to walk it in the dark.

Just yesterday evening when I was wheeling the garbage bin down my long sandy drive, a woman had emerged from the shadows, running towards me along the main road, a jogger dressed in a pink and yellow fluorescent singlet, white shorts and old running shoes. On her forehead was a headlight attached to a fluorescent band, the kind you buy in outdoor shops. With a glazed look of exertion she had pounded past on the gravel, staring ahead, then stopped, retraced her steps and stood on the verge, panting. 'Hi, I'm Kelly.' She gestured towards the headland. 'From up the road.'

Kelly was small and thin and fine-boned. She would once have been pretty, though her face now was taut and dry.

'Do you always run in the dark?'

'Most nights.'

'Isn't it dangerous?' I was squinting because the light on Kelly's forehead was shining into my eyes.

'Oh, there's very little traffic around here. And I've got three kids under seven. It's the only time I have for me.' And she adjusted the headlight, which had slipped down over one eye so that she looked like a maimed pirate.

'I'm Erica.'

'Yeah, I know, Lynnie told me. Good to meet ya, Erica—good to see someone in the old shack.' She tightened the strap on the headlight and shook her shoulders like an athlete ready to take up her position in the starting block. 'Well, see ya round.' And off she went, running in a steady stride towards the headland. And I lingered at the side of the road until she was out of sight. The vision of that slender maternal body receding into the dark was unsettling. Three children under seven and running, running. What if, like Irene, women kept on running and didn't turn back?

The labyrinth is a model of reversible destiny...

○

My son's father: Gabriel Priest. The son of a judge. The old man had tried to fondle me and if I couldn't avoid his groping embraces I would fold my shoulders in towards him so that my body was concave and he couldn't squeeze my breasts.

Gabe hated him.

When the money ran out from Ken's estate, Gabe and I found a squat in Redfern. My inheritance had been meagre: Ken had not owned the asylum cottage we lived in and had paid for many of the materials in the craft workshop out of his own pocket. The squat was a dilapidated two-storey terrace and Gabe, who had dropped out of art school, spread a big tarp over the only room that got any sunlight and set up an easel. I knew that his paints were expensive but Gabe said he had a mate who worked in a shop that sold art materials and stole them for him.

The narrow terrace was full of mould and leaking

gas. Strips of faded wallpaper hung from the walls and the house was built on clay which had shrunk in the long-running drought; a crack three centimetres wide opened up in the kitchen wall at the rear, and in winter it was draughty and cold. The cockroaches ran riot and every morning I wiped their black pinhead faeces from the chipped Formica benchtops. Upstairs we slept on a mattress on the floor with Daniel between us, his fine-limbed body curled into my back. By then he was almost three, and I worked nights behind a bar in the city serving cocktails to jittery young executives and their glassy-eyed girlfriends.

Gabe had an old blue station wagon and late one afternoon we were almost to the end of Cleveland Street when out of nowhere a drab grey delivery van roared up alongside and forced us over to the kerb. Two men leapt out, shabbily dressed, unshaven, tattooed and wild-eyed.

'Get out!' they screamed. 'Get out of the car!'

Gabe was stunned. He climbed out of the wagon and they each took one of his arms and pushed him roughly against the brick wall of a nearby warehouse. Their bodies were taut, their eyes frantic, and the tall one began to frisk Gabe, who stood there limp like a rag doll. My first reaction was to glance nervously into the back seat of the wagon where Daniel was strapped into a booster seat I had that morning bought at the Tempe tip shop. His plastic bottle of juice had rolled onto the floor of the car and was lying on old newspapers beside a pair of muddy sneakers, and staring down at the juice bottle I knew, suddenly, that these men were undercover police and they were looking for drugs. Then the short stocky one was in my face and ordering me against the wall. 'You're police, aren't you?' I said.

'What do you fucking think we are?' he hissed, and whipped out a badge from the pocket of his red flannelette shirt. He was wired, nervous and angry. They've received a tip-off, I thought, and it's beginning to dawn on them they've got the wrong car.

In swift, jerky movements he patted me down and pulled out the pockets of my jacket, but by this time he was half-hearted and going through the motions, though trembling still from the adrenaline rush of just minutes before. The tall one wrenched open the back of the wagon and began to fling things about. There was fear in his eyes and it occurred to me that they might have been expecting someone armed. Only the week before a madman, barefoot and stripped to the waist, had held up traffic just one street over from our squat, firing off a .22 rifle at random.

Furious at having blown it, they climbed back into the grey van and took off down the road. Gabe came over and put his arm around me. 'You okay, babe?' he asked. And then, 'Thank Christ we didn't have a joint on us.' But all I could think of was Daniel, and I opened the rear door of the wagon and leaned in. My baby was very still, unblinking and wide-eyed. Then he grinned. People would often remark on his composure as an infant.

'There's something about him,' they'd say.

Gabe was still shaking. We drove to a bottle shop, bought two bottles of cheap red, and went home to drink and calm our nerves.

The next morning, Gabe was gone. I waited three days and then I knew. How deep in was he? How in debt? How afraid? After two weeks I packed up our few things and wrote to my brother in Adelaide for money. By then Axel was in the final year of his medical degree and he drew on his inheritance to rescue me. He was the thrifty one, and it was unfair, but I had no one else.

With the money from Axel I paid the bond on an attic room in an unrenovated terrace in Surry Hills, but it was freshly painted and clean, though stifling in the summer heat. The room was tiny, with just a single bed and a clothes rack, and I bought a new single mattress for Daniel so that he could sleep on the floor beside my bed and I could stack the mattress against the wall during the day. One morning, carrying Daniel's stroller down the steep staircase, I lost my footing and fell, but landed on the big Labrador that liked to sleep at the foot of the stairs. With barely a grunt of protest it broke my fall while Daniel stood stock-still, halfway down the stairs, hanging on to a baluster. The old man who lived in one of the rooms below came out and offered to make me a cup of tea, an act of kindness that threatened to undo me. If Daniel had not been there and so obviously alarmed I might have wept in self-pity.

There were moments when I gazed into my son's eyes in rapture, but also at times in despair. We were too alone.

By this time I had day work. I had registered with an employment agency and they sent me to a position as a receptionist at the Palace, a small hotel in Victoria Street in Kings Cross. The job came with a warning that there was high staff turnover because of the eccentricity of its owner. That's all right, I thought: I grew up in an asylum; I'm used to eccentricity.

The Palace had been built in the 1890s but was known informally as the Marshall after its long-term owner, Lloyd Marshall, who was in his late seventies. Lloyd was tall and slim and stooped, with thinning ginger-grey hair, blood-shot eyes, chipped yellow teeth and wiry tufts of hair that sprouted from his ears. He was too mean to spend money on anything much, including the decrepit plumbing of his hotel that on some floors leaked and discoloured the walls. On most days he hung around the corridors, shadowing the staff, seedy and disgruntled. 'Just keeping an eye on my investment, girlie,' he'd say.

It soon became clear that it was Lloyd's policy to rent out rooms by the hour at the same tariff as overnight but I figured it was none of my business. Couples needed somewhere to rendezvous and it might as well be the Marshall. On some mornings the cleaners, two middle-aged Chilean women, would come to the office with a plastic bag of things left behind by patrons, and with avid haste Lloyd's long bony fingers would rummage through the bag looking for the sex toys that were sometimes there, and if he thought no-one was looking he would sniff at them: a pair of rubber manacles, fluorescent condoms with armadillo spikes, G-strings stiff with dried sperm, ribbed dildoes with gummy plastic sheaths.

One muggy afternoon in January the police raided the hotel. They claimed to have been told there was a de facto brothel operating there, and I lied and said Lloyd wasn't around even though I knew he had locked himself in the little room behind the reception desk that had a false door. I lied instinctively, stupidly. It was reckless and made me an accomplice to any scheme of Lloyd's that might have been in play. But it meant something to him. Thereafter, out of the blue, he would pat me on the shoulder and say, apropos of nothing, 'I can trust you, girlie. You're a good girl, aren't you?'

In this way Daniel and I made our life for the next two years. Apart from the raid the only real dramas at the Marshall were the shouting matches between Lloyd and his son when Warren came into the office to badger his father about money. Warren wanted Lloyd to sell the hotel to a developer so it could be demolished but Lloyd wouldn't budge. 'I can't trust that son of mine,' he'd say. 'He wants to do me down.' He even hinted that he thought Warren had prompted the police raid. His eyes narrowed: 'He's probably got them on the take. But I'll spike his guns, wait and see.'

One day Lloyd didn't come in, and then the next day

and the next, until late on the Friday afternoon Warren appeared and announced to the staff that Mr Marshall had died in his sleep. 'You,' he said, turning to me, 'can have two weeks' notice.' Why the animosity? I scarcely knew him. But within days I had picked up another job as a receptionist, this time in an upmarket boutique hotel at The Rocks, a converted warehouse. It may be that Warren had sensed something in his father's attitude to me because five months on, when old Marshall's will was read, I received a lawyer's letter to say that Lloyd had left me twenty thousand dollars.

I was blindsided. And felt obscurely ashamed. It was tainted money, and at the same time a blessing, enough at that time for the deposit on a small apartment. But it was a legacy with little logic. Lloyd had never even made a pass at me. And it wasn't as if he had been fond of Daniel. On those occasions when Daniel came in after school he would shrug and say: 'I see the brat's here.' There was no entitlement on my part; no apparent cause and effect, no hidden sentimental chord such as that he had once lost a daughter. I was not even a long-term employee. Everyone has some good instincts, Axel had said, even old Marshall. Perhaps, he mused, it had been ten thousand dollars for each year I had worked for him. Perhaps, I said, but couldn't help thinking that good instincts had nothing to do with it, rather something more primal, for I recollected that not long after Lloyd had died the barman in the downstairs bar, Paddy, told me that on one occasion, late at night when Lloyd had a few drinks in, he had become maudlin, and confided to Paddy that I bore a striking resemblance to his mother.

When I ran into Warren one day on the street he sneered: 'Lucky you, eh?' And I knew he believed the legacy was for services rendered, that I had pandered to the old man's appetites. I didn't bother to correct him. Let him think that. Let him resent that his father might have had a good time.

Just after Daniel started school, and before I had news of the legacy, we went to live in an old mansion in Potts Point. Every evening after work I would collect Daniel from after-school care and we would wait in the warm subtropical twilight for the bus to come by, and watch the bats flying home to roost in the park. On one of those evenings I ran into Brian Murnane. Brian was an Irishman who had taught me beginners' Greek in the first year of my abandoned degree. Occasionally he would lecture his novices on Plato to, as he said, give us an idea of what we could look forward to. (Enrolments were down and he needed to recruit us into a second year.) He would breeze into the seminar room smelling of alcohol and lecture with bold declarative flourishes in his rasping Belfast accent. 'All you need to know is in Plato,' he would say. '*Anamnesis*, meaning recollection. Learning is a way of finding a path to what we already know but have forgotten, so wake up.' And: 'The human mind is potentially connected to an obscure elsewhere, some other place, before time. And where is this place? That's for you to find out.' This, at least, is what I remember, what I *recollect*.

In the old-fashioned lingo of the day Brian had seduced me, though I had been willing, curious and eager. But the affair had been short-lived because all too soon I had fallen under the spell of Gabriel Priest.

Brian was living now with a woman, Rose Tooley, who rented out a room in the Italianate villa in Potts Point that she had inherited from her mother. When he learned of my situation Brian suggested that I move in with him and Rose—not, I thought, without ulterior motive, though I was wrong about that. As I was soon to discover, he was besotted with Rose.

Rose worked as the librarian in an exclusive girls' school where her salary would have been modest and she had expensive tastes, or maybe it was just that Brian had persuaded her to an act of charity. Rose was twelve years older than Brian, a woman with a long, narrow face, high cheekbones, thin lips and small teeth that looked unusually sharp. She wore her hennaed hair in a pageboy cut and favoured leopard-skin leggings and ballet slippers. When in a good mood she would invite me for cocktails. 'I'm a pagan,' she would purr, 'aren't I, darling?' Nibbling at Brian's ear and squeezing his buttocks with her long slender fingers.

For a time I found myself drawn to Rose, as a study rather than a friend. Rose was 'womanly', or at least that was Brian's word for her. She had rules about being a woman and judged her own sex by the quality of two things: what she called their lingerie, and their shoes. She had several expensive nightdresses that she called negligees—diaphanous cotton, black or red silk, lavender muslin with sprigs of blue flowers, or a more vampish satin. She was profligate with shoes, and vain, and because her feet were large she often succumbed to the temptation to buy them in a size too small for her. These were then discarded as 'unsuitable' with the excuse that they were the wrong colour, or had an irritating strap. I benefited from this as my feet were small and narrow and the discards fitted me. Rose took pride in dispensing fashion largesse, making a fuss of my 'teeny little feet'. Look at her teeny little feet, Brian, she would say with contrived good humour.

One evening Rose asked me about my mother. 'You should find out about her,' she said. 'Aren't you curious?'

'She drowned. Two years after she left us.'

'Drowned where?'

As if it mattered. 'Near Lismore. She tried to cross a flooded road and her car was swept into the river.' Irene had gone to live in a commune outside the town and was on her way home from a local nursery. When emergency services retrieved the body they found the car was full of flowering plants, a detail that has stayed with me, so that at odd times those plants have invaded my dreams, their sodden petals floating on the surface of the murky water.

'How ghastly.' Rose shuddered. 'Can't stand Lismore. Dreary little place.'

'Oh, I don't know,' Brian said, in an awkward effort at tact. 'I quite like it.'

To my relief they segued into a discussion about small rural towns and the ones that did or did not have charm, a conversation that culminated in a theatrical account by Rose of how she had lost her virginity one night in the middle of a football oval in Beechworth. 'My dears, he was *huge*, but you know, I didn't bleed, there was no hymen. A shrink I knew said he thought I might have been molested, but, you know, very young, like three or something, too young to remember it.'

Brian appeared to have heard this before; at least, he didn't react. Rose's self-absorption was welcome to me, for I did not care to discuss my mother with anyone. If Irene had not drowned when she did it was possible she might have returned to claim her children, which is what Axel and I liked to think. But Ken had decided not to tell us of our mother's death, not at the time, anyway, only much later. How could a psychiatrist, of all people, inflict such cruelty on his children? If we had known she was dead we wouldn't have been haunted by the possibility of her return, would not have kept a watch out for her slim, long-legged figure, her burnished chestnut hair that hung with a thick wavy weight on her shoulders. Sometimes, when I glimpsed one of the asylum nurses at a distance, walking towards me across the fine lawns, I would imagine for a moment that it was Irene returning from a shopping expedition in the town. Later, Axel would defend Ken, arguing that he had sought to protect us, that the worst he was culpable of was a misguided idea of the value of hope. No, I had said, with rare vehemence, he was wrong, and in a spasm of angry mockery had quoted Reverend Harwood: *It is a mistake ever to second-guess the Lord.* But Axel had shaken his head and turned away.

Brian became my friend, though not always a reliable one. Drinking was his sport, mostly red wine but he was fond too of ouzo and brandy. It was almost a point of honour with him never to be entirely sober—but it was like that then; we all drank more than we ever would again. Neither Rose nor Brian bothered to cook and seemed only to snack on whatever happened to be lying around. Brian would pounce on leftovers from food I had prepared and say, 'Mmm, may I?' But he was good with Daniel and would take him to the park at weekends when he had slept off his hangover, and they would kick a soccer ball around. In that department he seemed to have a surprising amount of skill, picked up no doubt on the streets of Belfast, and was in general more co-ordinated than his gangly frame would suggest. His interest in Daniel, his casual kindness, endeared him to me more than the carnal intimacy we had shared in the past.

Even now I can recall the smell of Rose's house, that smell of mould and old money. But outside our bedroom window, mine and Daniel's, was an old maple tree, and from my bed I could see the full extent and reach of it, from the moss around its base to the cluster of fine branches at the top. And I believe that tree sustained me, for almost from the first day the tree and I entered into a relationship of looking. I would sit on the edge of the bed and gaze at the tree and the tree looked back at me, a living thing personal both in its proximity and its loveliness, and yet impersonal in its immutable groundedness, its conformity to the dictates of the form within the seed: the growing, the thriving, the lush leafiness, the autumnal red and gold, the drying up and shedding, the prodigal disposal of its own bloom, the revelation of a nest in its uppermost branches when its limbs were bare, and then the slow budding of the leaf and the cycle beginning again. There was not a day when it didn't change, and I saw myself in it: not stuck, not a mendicant in that old house, but a young woman in transition.

After a year Brian was appointed to a fellowship in Melbourne, and Rose shut up the house and followed him. I didn't hear from either of them again, though Brian had said that Daniel and I must come and visit. To my surprise, I missed him. In his jealousy, his defiant obsessiveness, Gabriel Priest had shut me off from everyone, but Brian had been kind to me. In Rose's house we had become friends, and in an odd, surprising and unsexual way had struck up a rapport. I worried that he drank too much and sensed, even then, that he would drink himself to death, looking perhaps for that obscure elsewhere, that other place before time.

Another day, another book to burn. The days are cool again and the shack is without insulation. In the evenings I light a fire in the living-room fireplace, which is shallow and smokes; it spits embers onto the rug and the first billow of smoke stings my eyes.

This morning I unpacked some of my son's books and stacked them at random on shelves fixed to the wall by a previous owner. I have made a pact with myself not to look within any of the books but this morning I was tempted by an old leather-bound copy of Robert Louis Stevenson's *Kidnapped* that I recognised as having belonged to my father. I sat on one of the wooden boxes, opened the book and with my father's voice echoing in my head began to read. Ken had liked to read aloud, a practice intolerably tedious as far as Axel and I were concerned; we would roll our eyes at one another, captives for the moment of his vain pursuit to reel us in to his boyhood pleasures. *I will begin the story of my adventures with a certain morning early in the month of June, the year of grace 1751, when I took the key for the last time out of the door of my father's house. The sun began to shine upon the summit of the hills as I went down the road; and by the time I had come as far as the manse, the blackbirds were whistling in the garden lilacs, and the mist that hung around the valley in the time of the dawn was beginning to arise and die away.*

Was ever a story begun so directly and with such

artless conviction? And all those years later I too had read aloud to Daniel, every night when we lived out of a tent in camping grounds, driving for months up the east coast, a time when I schooled him myself, clever kid that he was. He was an anxious child and the reading soothed him. It was then that he began his fantastical drawings and could not go to sleep at night until he had completed at least one. Even though, at the time, I had packed hastily I had thrown some books into a box and at night he would draw in their margins, and sometimes on the flyleaf; would put his stamp on them, as if to take possession of the thing he loved. I ought not to have allowed it but so artful were these miniatures that I came to prize them and would look forward to the next one, and the next. They offered me a window into his psyche. One night he pointed to an intricate constellation of crenellated towers he had sketched and said: 'This is where my father lives.' And I ought to have drawn him out, and asked him to describe this place, but my heart sank in my chest from the pity of it. I was young, and not wise, struck dumb by the defiant hope in his eyes.

Daniel's favourite story was also one of my father's books, Ballantyne's *The Coral Island*, and I suspected that this was a fantasy, an imaginary self: he was its young hero, Ralph Rover, shipwrecked on an idyllic island and smart enough to outwit the savages who inhabited it. And for all that time he, Daniel, had been shipwrecked with his mother, on the run from a man who threatened them, not his father who had abandoned them, but another man. I had made a bad choice, had fallen into a sexual thrall, something no mother can afford other than with the father of her child, and perhaps not even then. And Daniel, with a child's intuition, had felt the cord begin to fray; had felt alone, twice abandoned.

But now, as I read, here in the shack behind the dunes, time is annulled. *I will begin the story of my adventures with a certain morning early in the month of June…* And Daniel is a boy again, and we are driving up the coast and singing together in the car. We are alive within these pages and there is such a thing as a year of grace.

○

I have come to feel that this house is my web. On some days I am the spider, on other days the fly. Like both I exist only to survive through the ritual of feeding. In the case of the spider the form of the web is incidental, a by-product of its predatory instinct. And it's the form of things that can disorient me, times when the everyday, its smallest detail, can seem uncanny and the most mundane object strange. A loaf of bread on a wooden carving board. Why that shape? That size? That density? It's the form of things that is uncanny, not their function.

My days are full of undefined lack, but they are not dull, though to the observer they might appear so. Each detail of each day is defined by my impending visit to my son, not the previous visit, which I contrive to not dwell on, but the next, which is never without potential. Though all now is static, something surely must shift, for this is in the nature of things. In the city it was impossible to sustain this faith; the very flurry and insistence of constant movement around me had the perverse effect of its opposite—amid the frenetic movement what lay beneath the surface seemed petrified. Now the placid surface of the coast suggests not resignation but waiting. Here we gaze constantly at the weather, and weather is volatile.

And this shack is in sympathy with the weather: its refusal of conventional form, its rough extensions, the fact that no two windows or doors are alike, its asymmetric nooks, its one long hallway and two foreshortened ones, its dated picture rails. Nothing definitive and yet not ugly, not bound but flagrantly improvised. Not subject to renovation and so wholly heterogeneous that it cannot be improved upon other than with a little paint over the bare Masonite walls of the two small bedrooms. At least this was my initial supposition. But when I painted one of the walls it somehow looked worse, absurdly shiny and new, cheap and dishonest. Leave me alone, the shack says. You bought me because I am as I am: in no way a statement, an expression of style. A dwelling of accidental charm.

This morning I am headed for the lagoon and my daily walk up the long ocean beach. It's a season of low tides and the smell of the seaweed is neither rank nor pungent but aromatic, a heady blend of salt and briny sweetness. On the wide expanse of exposed sandbar by the edge of the lagoon I find a large bird's egg nestled in a depression in the sand and covered in black streaky markings that look like the imprint of seaweed on the shell. The egg is exposed to predators and I imagine the sea sweeping in over it and the egg barely moving, listing a little in its hollow in the direction of the incoming tide.

Back on the road I can see the postman parked in his van beside my letterbox. In the box there is a letter from Axel. He has written to me before this but I have burned his letters unopened. Perhaps he has intuited this because this time he has written on the outside of the envelope and my glance cannot escape the words: 'Please, Erica, I am not the enemy.' No, he is not the enemy but I do not welcome any display of sympathy, least of all from Axel, to whom I might have been a more loving sister. We had quarrelled over his wife, who had made plain her disdain for me, and what she referred to as my irresponsible child-rearing practices. Axel had attempted to make the peace but my pride rebuffed him. He owes me nothing. I must deal with this alone. Meanwhile, far from being known to me, my closest familiar, my son, is now an unknown. On each visit to Daniel I travel towards this unknown; I do not know what I will find when I arrive and this alone makes the pain of these confrontations bearable.

o

Daniel is mute. Not since he shouted 'Rubbish!' on my first visit has he uttered a word.

The air in this room is vile; it smells of metal and the acrid ammonia tang of fresh concrete.

One day the younger of the two guards had winked at me as I left and said: 'Not much of a talker, is he?'

Today Daniel's thick black hair has been shaved to stubble and his eyes are bloodshot.

I begin carefully. 'I have something to tell you and I hope you won't be upset.'

Not a flicker.

'I have written to the prison governor, Daniel. I've asked for permission to send you some oil pastels and some drawing paper.' I take a deep breath before the lie. 'I haven't had a reply yet but I think they'll agree.' In fact they have refused but I have taken it up with Jodie of the prisoners' support group and I will write to the governor every week until he grants permission.

At the word 'pastels' Daniel closes his eyes as if in pain. Then he shakes his head as if to say: I'm done with that. His hands rest on the table, fine boned hands, well formed, the hands of his father. I try not to look at them and look instead at the clock on the wall, a plain round face, white with black hands, the kind of clock you see at IKEA stores. Cheap to replace if smashed, though it's set high on the wall and your aim would have to be good.

On the drive home I recall the day—he might have been eleven—when Daniel asked me what his name meant. I knew this, had looked it up when he was born. I told him: 'God is my judge.'

'Is that bad?' he asked.

'We don't believe in God,' I said. 'You must be your own judge.'

Until it was too late I had not known about the woman, the woman he was obsessed with, the woman he had painted over and over, dismembering her body in a series of drawings of her body parts: the curve of her hip, the volume of her breasts, the roundness of her elbow, the tilt of her chin, the perfect circle of her navel. Drawing after drawing, no detail spared: the mole on her left shoulder, the scar above her top lip. Had she been afraid when she was confronted by this disaggregation that covered the walls of his studio? Whatever the reason, when she abandoned him for someone else he slashed his canvases and poured kerosene around the perimeter of his studio, a room in a warehouse that was being converted into apartments. I understood his fury. I understood that either his work or the loved one had to be annihilated. And, in a sense, he had chosen self-immolation, but blindly, and five people who had moved into the new apartments above his studio had died, among them a young couple not long returned from their honeymoon.

Homicidal negligence. *The judge had described it as a monstrous act of egotism, as if nothing mattered other than the defendant's work, even in the act of destroying it. And all Daniel could say when first I saw him after his arrest was: 'I have been my own judge, mother.'*

And now it's the faces of the honeymoon couple, laughing in colour on the front pages of the newspapers, that are etched now in my mind's eye, there to flicker, off and on, like half-resurrected ghosts. Had Daniel known they were in the building? He had refused to answer this question, as if it bore no relation to the necessity of the deed. He had refused to say anything more at all.

o

Tonight I eat late and drink more than usual. There are some nights when it's best not to sleep, for fear I will dream again of Daniel. In these dreams he is always a figure just out of reach: a baby abandoned in a straw-lined crib; a knight in armour on a black horse careening away from me; a small boy immersed in roiling surf up to his neck, a grinning, disembodied head bobbing above the waves. So painful are these phantoms that I open my eyes in a blood rush of panic and with a rumble in my chest like the wheels of a tumbrel. Then I must get up, and leave the house, and walk up the steep hill to prowl along the grassy headland.

Tonight the sound of the ocean is unfamiliar, its slow rhythmic surge more like a quickened throb. Garra Nalla is dark at night and I must rely on my torch as there is only one streetlight. I have learned from Lynnie Gittus that the council once proposed to install street lighting, along with kerbs and guttering, but the residents organised a petition against improvements; they do not want to live in anything resembling a suburb; they want to preserve an illusion of the primitive, the unspoiled. It means that the verges are grassy and pocked with shallow bandicoot hollows and the gutters are roughly excavated swales, deep and lined with sharp-edged stones that sprout weeds.

Beside the edge of the cliff, just a metre away from the blowhole, my left foot drops into a sinkhole created by the roots of an old macrocarpa cypress, and as my ankle twists I fall forward, and then sideways, my foot caught in the hole, my shoe wedged between the roots. Bracing for the pain I wrench free, then hoist myself up and limp back down the hill. I am lucky not to have broken my leg.

Inside the house I can't be bothered to undress. Instead I lie on the couch and cover myself with an old Guatemalan shawl. I would like to be rid of this shawl, which reminds me of a brutal love affair that left me with a broken nose and two broken ribs; then again, on nights like this I would like to be rid of everything. I could strip the house until I have only a table, a chair and a bed. I could take all of Daniel's books out onto the sandy gap, the tufts of coarse grass and the yellow capeweed, and burn them in an immense bonfire that would light up the dunes. Or I could just lie still and let the cortisol surge through my veins in a tsunami of dread. But my ankle continues to throb and after a while I lift myself up and limp down the hallway to rummage in the bathroom cupboard for codeine. The body makes its demands with no regard for the past. I have fallen down a hole, I have bruised my leg, I am alive and the blood flows in my veins, in the body that has carried me here.

I hobble into the sunroom, and rest my foot on a low stool. A book has arrived in the mail, a book that promises to be a compendium of labyrinth designs. A London artist has installed a different labyrinth in each of the city's 270 Underground stations, though these installations are of necessity small designs silk-screened onto enamel plates, fired and then fixed to station walls. There is no question of walking them. The choice—the variety—is bewildering, and I push the book aside and practise, again, drawing the seed pattern by hand with a pen. This is the pattern to which I keep returning: the nub of the cervix, the runnels of the womb. But my drawing is poor, the proportions distorted. Daniel would often laugh at my attempts to draw anything, he who had the sure hand of his father. But under the pool of lamplight my hand moves now on auto pilot while my ankle throbs, page after blank page inscribed with lopsided ovoid shapes while I wait for the relief of the opioid and the unthinking flow that will achieve some semblance of symmetry. Over and over until the swallows stir in their nest and light appears at the window.

But this trawling at night, this taking of endless notes, is only a postponement of the inevitable, of the task itself. Though a labyrinth is in no way as complicated as a maze, when I study the designs online the mathematics of the task are daunting: the proportions must be finely calculated with a compass and hard edge. I who am too impatient to weigh the ingredients of a recipe with accuracy and cannot wrap a present with any degree of finesse cannot, with confidence, envisage how I might become my own geometer. When I look at the diagrams, the dotted lines of precise calibration, the constellation of numbers and decimal points, iron markers driven into the ground, outlines sprayed with white paint, esoteric talk about sacred geometry and the significance of the number twelve, I am deflated. I am the prisoner of an idea with no path to its realisation. Were it not for the dream I would not persist, but for now I remain its captive.

o

It's three days before I can walk again to the beach. At low tide the sandbank at the centre of the lagoon is exposed, but the tide is on the turn and the waters of the ocean are flowing in through the barway and filling the narrow channel on the northern side. A white egret has alighted on the sandbank and with thin black legs is prowling the edge in a slow stalking tread, hoping to pluck a mullet from the murky swirl of incoming water.

A woman in a wetsuit is stroking her red kayak along the lagoon. Her cropped black hair is streaked with grey and she is thickset, with broad shoulders and a deep tan. She moves with a powerful grace that is mesmerising and is so obviously at home on the choppy water, so untroubled by the swirl of the current, that she is like some large-bodied bird that has scattered the smaller ones to the fringes of the lagoon. And while I look on she strokes her way to the edge of the lagoon and pulls the kayak up onto its pebbly shore, handling it deftly as if it were made of balsa wood and tying it to a spindly tree where other boats are moored. 'Hi there,' she says, and waves, before disappearing into the boobialla where a narrow sandy track winds steeply up the rocky face of the headland.

I turn back towards the shack. In the pocket of my vest is a letter, a letter that has given me hope. On my way to the beach I had opened the letterbox at the end of my sandy drive to find an envelope with the familiar government logo of the Department of Corrective Services. *Permission has been granted to send the art materials nominated in your previous correspondence to the prisoner Daniel Priest. It is hoped that the specified materials may have a pacifying effect on the prisoner and deter any attempts at self-harm. These materials must be posted via normal mail and they will be inspected upon arrival. There are severe penalties for...* Before walking to the beach I had returned to the house to make my arrangements, and for the first time in months I allow myself to experience a mild elation.

o

Thursday, and I wait in the concrete and steel visitors' room.

There is only silence, the usual quiet in this room other than the warders coughing or the slight scuffing sound of their steel-capped boots as they shift their weight from one foot to another.

When Daniel is ushered through the door I feel there is something different about him, almost a swagger. After getting the letter granting permission for the art materials I had ordered them online the same day, a box of fifty Sennelier oil pastels and a ream of thick art paper, and had them dispatched by courier. By now he would have received them, unless for some reason they have been withheld. Could it be that he is drawing again? That his mood has improved?

'I sent you some pastels in the mail.'

He nods.

'Have they given them to you?'

Still meeting my gaze he reaches into the sleeve of his orange boilersuit to extract a green oil crayon which he holds up between us, brandishing it like a trophy.

My heart lurches. 'Good,' I say.

'Yes, good,' he repeats. He lowers the pastel, as if contemplating it, and then, although it is solid and the size of a thick cigar, he snaps it in half. One half he lays on the table between us, careful to set it in a straight line. Then he puts the other half in his mouth and begins to chew on it.

I lower my voice to a whisper. 'I hope you're enjoying that, Daniel.'

With a sudden shift he rocks back on his chair and sticks out his tongue, which is now a greenish black.

I look down to where the pointed end of the crayon sits between us like a small missile. After a while I pick it up and put it in the pocket of my jacket, but at this he groans and begins to beat his head against the steel table. The table gives

65

off a clanking boom, then a dull vibrating thrum. He grasps
the sides of the table as if attempting to shake it but it's bolted
to the floor. I become aware that one of the warders is moving
towards us but I look up at him and, raising my hands, palms
outward in an attitude of surrender, shake my head. He stops,
and takes a step back, for Daniel is quiet now, slumped in his
chair with his eyes closed.

The hatred of the mother who is not enough, who is not
the longed-for father.

o

The Duncans' house is a brutal cube of concrete set high
on the grassy headland. On a sunny day the light glares off
its bone-white walls but when the sky is overcast the cube
looks drab, like an exposed bunker where at any moment
the long grey barrel of a field gun might be wheeled out
onto the terrace.

Frances Duncan has invited me to a party. Lynnie
Gittus must have told her about me, for one morning
Frances knocked on my door and introduced herself.
Hugh and I would so like it if you could join us, she said.

On the night of the party I put on a dress, something
I haven't worn in a long time, and walk up the hill to the
headland with a sense that I am out of place and should
turn back. But in the past week, secure behind the dunes,
something in me has shifted and I have begun to crave
human company, open to distraction and yet fearful of it.
I feel I must think of Daniel every minute of the day, must

hold him in the net of my thoughts for his own protection, must not lose myself in any distraction, other than the labyrinth, for then I might lose *him*, in the way that a child might float away on the tide when its guardian is distracted. I am all he has.

The massive double doors of the Duncan cube give the house the air of a fortress. Ten feet tall and painted a bright blue, they open into a wide courtyard with a white pebbled floor and lime-washed walls. Along the walls are huge terracotta urns with lemon trees and in the centre of the courtyard flames are leaping from a cast-iron brazier. The courtyard is full of people, mostly middle-aged, all of them lit by a strobe light that emanates from the northern wall of the courtyard, a rectangular grotto where red bulbs have been installed in the shape of a cross that pulsates with a gory neon glow.

Frances Duncan appears and takes my arm. She is flushed and seems unsteady in her white stiletto sandals. 'So lovely to see you. Thank you for coming. Do you know anyone here?'

'No, I don't think so.'

'Then you must meet Lewis.' And she ushers me through the crowd to a corner where a tall, lean man with closely cropped grey hair is standing by himself. 'Erica, this is Lewis. Lewis, Erica. Now excuse me, both of you, while I get some more canapés.'

I have seen Lewis Eames on the beach, walking his black kelpie, and we have nodded but never spoken. I know from Lynnie that he is an architect who works from home, though Lynnie does not think well of him. 'He's a recluse, that one. Thinks he's better than the rest of us. You won't get any change out of him.'

We make the usual small talk about weather and speak of the drought, and how, if the rains don't come, I will have to buy in water. Lewis tells me about Dinny, the weed-control man who has a water business on the side, and I say, yes, I know about Dinny, and there is that awkward moment in a casual encounter, a mute pause, when one of you might decide to disengage and move on—and it's then that a woman approaches. Lewis gives her a cold stare. 'I'll just refresh my glass,' he says, and disappears into the throng of bodies around the brazier.

The woman raises her eyebrows and snorts. 'He's scared of me,' she says. 'We had a fling once and it ended badly.' She adjusts the fold of her floral sarong, which has slipped almost to her nipples to reveal a deep, bronzed cleavage, and her small dark eyes burrow into me as if I am prey. And I recognise her. It's the woman with the red kayak who greeted me beside the lagoon.

'I'm Diana Crosland,' she says, 'and I know who you are. You're the woman who's renting that wreck behind the sandhills.'

'Actually, I bought it.'

'No? Seriously?'

'Yes, seriously.'

'Well, welcome to our little sandpit.' She raises her

glass in a mock toast and then, glancing across to where the neon cross is blinking from its gruesome niche: 'That bloody thing's getting on my nerves,' she says. 'Let's go inside.' We begin to push our way through the crush but Diana is soon greeted effusively by another woman who behaves as if I am not there. Alone and feeling awkward I edge my way through the crowd towards a set of immense glass doors that slide open to reveal the Duncans' living room. It's empty, a long rectangular space that looks and feels like an art gallery, with white walls and clinical all-white furniture. At the centre is an enormous white couch that billows out in a cloud of leather, seeming almost to float above the floor in lush curves of expensive tumescence. On either side are two tall floor lamps carved in the shape of stylised herons, each with a linen lampshade caught in its beak. A plate-glass wall looks out onto the ocean where waves are surging towards the house as if, at any moment, they might sweep into the room and break across the polished concrete floor. The house might be a boat perched on a reef.

Frances Duncan enters through the glass doors. She is carrying an empty tray which she sets down on a granite bench. She hesitates, and with a glazed expression begins to fill the tray with tiny canapés, so small and intricately wrought that they look like trout-fishing lures. When the tray is full she gives me one of her unfocussed smiles. 'So glad you could come,' she says, then picks up the tray and stumbles out into the courtyard.

I see that she is vulnerable, that she is gliding through this party like a ghost. I must go, I think. Everything here is too white.

At the big blue doors of the courtyard I am accosted by a muscular man in his sixties who introduces himself as Hugh Duncan and grasps my elbow. 'Hi there,' he says, 'you're a foxy little piece. We should have a coffee sometime.'

'I don't think so.' I jerk my elbow away from him and he grins and releases his grip.

Out on the road the air is blessedly cool. A light breeze rises from the water. I tread carefully down the shadowy hill, using my phone to light a path. When I open the door to the shack I pause for a moment on the threshold to look at the things in my kitchen, to reassure myself of a quality I can't name. I had forgotten how unsettling, even disturbing the totems of other people's lives can be: the red neon cross, the floating white couch, the lamps like frozen herons.

o

At the weekends carloads of youths park at the turning circle beside the lagoon and carouse in the sand dunes. The gap, my bare stretch of tufted sand, is littered with empty cans of beer and mixer drinks. I gather them into a rubbish bag and dump them in the recycling bin. Late last night one of the cans hit a window and I flung back the covers in a fury and went out to investigate. But no one was there, though I could hear voices murmuring in the dunes.

On my morning walk, Lynnie beckons me from across the road. 'Coffee, love?'

Inside she hands me a steaming mug and comes straight to the point. 'I was wondering,' she says, 'if you might need any help in the house. In the garden and that.'

'Are you looking for more work, Lynnie?'

'No, not me, I've got my hands full as it is. It's just that Ray's niece, Lexie, will be leaving school at the end of the year. There's no work for her in the district and she'll have to move to the city, but she can't afford the move and needs to save up. Her dad's just been made redundant in the mine and her mum works part-time at the old people's home at Juno Park. It's a vicious circle for the young. What can they do? It's not fair. No wonder they end up on ice.'

'I'm sorry, Lynnie, but I really don't need any help. There's only me.'

'I know, love. I'm just putting it out there. Lexie's been working after school in the local bakery but they've just given her a week's notice. Not because she isn't a good kid but times are tough and they're just not selling as much.'

Ray is sitting in his usual spot on the veranda in the big wicker chair, wrapped in his blanket. 'Eh?' he bellows. 'What's that about Lexie?'

'Just telling Erica,' Lynnie shouts back.

'Nothing to tell about that little slut. I know what she

gets up to in the sandhills with those other idiots. She's a useless piece of work, that one.' And then the tinny high-pitched ring of his alarm clock. Lynnie grimaces and I pretend not to have heard it.

On the way out Ray looks up and grunts. 'You again.'

'Your wife invited me.'

'Well, don't come back.'

Lynnie turns to me with a pleading expression. 'Please don't take offence, love. Nothing personal.'

'Don't you apologise for me, you old bitch.'

I glare at him. *You pathetic fool.* I stifle an impulse to snatch the alarm clock and pitch it into the ferns on the empty block that lies between us. Instead I walk to the edge of the veranda and the steps leading down to the gate, and run a hand across my scalp; it feels as if a moth has dropped into my hair from under the eaves, or a flying beetle has entangled itself.

In the afternoon I walk up the hill to Lewis Eames' house, a two-storey mud-brick rectangle with a pitched roof surrounded by banksias. Through the window of his studio I can see him working at his drafting table. I knock on the door and he gets up. 'Hello,' he says, 'out for a walk?' He is pleasant enough but does not invite me in.

I get straight to the point. 'I'm going to build a labyrinth in my garden and I wondered if you would be willing to advise me.'

'What do you mean, build?' He is softly spoken.

I hesitate, my confidence faltering. 'I'm not sure. There seem to be some complex mathematics involved, beyond my capability at least.' This comes out sounding bad.

'I could look at the site,' he says.

'Well, perhaps you'd like to come for a drink.'

He hesitates. 'I could manage that.'

Late afternoon on the following day I watch as he turns into my sandy drive, punctually, at five. I open the side door and wave to indicate that the entrance is not where you would expect to find it. He approaches slowly, wearing a broad-brimmed straw hat, and pauses at the entrance. 'I like these old shacks,' he says. 'They know why they're here and what they're for.' He gazes up at the guttering. 'And I like your wide eaves. You'd expect that whoever built this place would have economised on something like that.'

I invite him in and he takes off his hat and puts it on the kitchen table in a considered way that suggests he has chosen the exact right spot on the table for hat-laying. He leans back against the table, arms crossed, while I fill the coffee machine with water.

'Are you working on a house at the moment?' I ask.

'No, a surf club. Up the coast, at Wynton.'

Wynton is a town famous for its annual surf carnival.

'Don't they already have a clubhouse?'

'Of a kind. But the old one's decrepit, full of asbestos.

The town's grown and they're cashed up, so now they want something flash.' He peers at me over his glasses. 'A temple to the mindless preoccupation of the locals with walking on water.'

'You don't surf?'

'Certainly not. I'm a city boy.'

While I prepare a drinks tray he strolls over to my bookcases on the far wall. His gaze moves steadily from shelf to shelf until he stops and picks out a slim paperback. 'Hmm, Leonard Cohen, eh?'

'One of my son's books.'

'You like him?'

'I've never read him.'

'I knew a woman once.' He pauses. 'She advertised for a soulmate on one of those online dating sites. She had a list of requirements and at the top it said'—and with his right index finger he draws an invisible line in the air—'must love Leonard Cohen.'

'Is that how you met her?'

'As a matter of fact it was.' He opens the book at random and reads aloud, something about a man with blood on his arm and the warmth of a bird. Lewis raises his head and looks across at me with a cocked eyebrow. 'What does that mean?'

I shake my head.

'She insisted I watch a DVD of one of his concerts.'

'You didn't like?'

'I recognised the type. An insider pretending to be an

outsider. Fooling the crowd.'

I register the note of grievance but say nothing; this is not the conversation I had imagined us having. I lift up the drinks tray and nod in the direction of the terrace. He opens the side door for me and I carry the tray outside and set it down on the outdoor table.

'Let me show you around the park,' I say, pointing to the expanse of flat sandy ground that abuts the sand dunes.

'Well, you've certainly got enough room,' he says. 'How big do you envisage this thing being?'

'I'm not sure.'

'You don't have a plan?'

'I have too many plans—possible plans, that is. I think I need to talk it through with someone practical.'

Under the shade of the eaves we settle on my old canvas chairs and look out across to where the sea is withdrawing from the raked surface of the beach. In the past year the slopes of the sandhills have eroded into vertical cliff faces two metres high, and the beach is littered with grey driftwood and thick rubbery ribbons of bull kelp.

'You realise that when the sea rises this area is liable to be submerged.'

'Yes, but not for a long time.'

'You don't want your labyrinth to last?'

'It will last long enough. For me.'

'So…' He pauses, drawing the word out. 'Got something you want to show me?'

'Not yet.'

He looks surprised, as well he might. He is thinking that I might be a little flaky, or that it's just a pitch to get him into my bed. 'How about materials?'

'I think I need to decide on a design first.'

'Well, probably best if you begin to think about materials. You can only build from materials that are accessible, and presumably within your budget. I imagine some designs would demand materials that might be hard to source around here, or expensive to import.'

Of course, this is how the practical man or woman thinks. Start with the material and work back to the design. Dreamers begin with the design and then find that the world won't accommodate it. Or them.

'Well,' I say, 'given the work you do I imagine you're familiar with local materials.'

He shrugs. 'Depends. You could use concrete and paint the pattern over it with outdoor paint. It would weather over time and then you refresh it. Or you could use polymer concrete, which is more permanent. The polymer is an overlay, like glue, that bonds to the concrete underneath. Your pattern is scored into the concrete with diamond-bladed tools and the polymer is applied over the top. But that's expensive.'

'I don't like concrete. In any form.'

'Not pretty enough?'

I let this condescension pass. 'I'd rather use earth or stone, or a combination of both.'

'Well, there are two quarries around here I could direct you to. If you give me some paper I'll draw you a map.'

I go inside to find paper and pen, and with deft, authoritative strokes he sketches me a rudimentary map and I see that he has nice hands. 'Try these,' he says, and doesn't offer to accompany me. Instead he drains his glass in the way of one making a decisive gesture and says he is going away soon for a month and he will get back to me when he returns. While he's away I can think about what it is I want and he'll think about whether he is the right person for the job.

'Well, that's good of you,' I say, even though it feels like a brush-off. 'I'll get your hat.'

He waits for me outside and when I return he is staring at me in a shrewd way. 'I should tell you that I know who you are, Erica.'

'Really. Who am I?'

'You're Daniel Priest's mother.'

So that's why he came for a drink. Curiosity.

'I did some work earlier in the year on the old court-house. In Darlinghurst. When they raised the roof they brought me in as a consultant. During the trial. I saw you come in through the main entrance. Several times.'

'I see.'

'Don't worry. I won't be telling anyone. It's nobody's business but yours.'

He puts on his hat, adjusting it at a rakish angle.

I watch him stroll down the dusty drive and when he reaches the road I collapse into a deck chair and look blankly out to sea. The dusk begins to fold in around me and the air cools. It's a clear night; the stars are out early; a small red cloud sits above the horizon. The black swans fly in and settle at the edge of the lagoon on the shallow brackish water, feeding with their heads immersed so that they look like small deformed sea creatures.

Later, I am unable to sleep. The memory of that courtroom. The face of the mother of the young woman who died. I lie in my bed, still as a corpse until two-thirty in the morning. Then I get up, make tea and sit at my laptop to scroll mindlessly through my notes. When, around five-thirty, a nimbus of dawn light begins to show around the edge of my blinds, I return to bed, bleary-eyed, and fall into a hallucinatory dream.

I am in the highlands, walking alone along a duck-board raised above swampy turf. I turn a corner and there, in a mossy clearing, is a lake, its surface so calm and still that I feel I might walk home on it. Around the lake's rocky rim a narrow path has been cut through alpine bush and the sinewy roots of trees lie exposed in the dirt. In the distance a mountain peak rises out of a pale grey mist, its flinty crag reflected in the water. There is something here that I need to remember, and I close my eyes to imprint the scene on my brain so that when I wake—for I know I am dreaming—I will recall it. But when I open my eyes the water begins to agitate, to ripple and surge, forming and reforming into the ghostly image of two distended faces floating on its surface, faces of the young couple who died in Daniel's inferno. Their heads are ballooning outwards, their hair on fire, and as I look on, the faces begin to break up, their eyes and smiling mouths rippling across the surface of the water, drifting and rippling until all trace of them is spent against the rocky shore, and the lake is restored to a frozen calm.

o

'What are these, Daniel?'

From behind the zip of his boilersuit Daniel has produced a sheaf of papers and is laying them out, with some ceremony, on the steel table. He looks up, his head tilted towards me, his dark eyes a challenge.

The drawings are in charcoal and the first is a highly detailed drawing of a scorpion. The second, an equally detailed drawing of a fly. The third, a huntsman spider.

'You draw what you see?'

He nods. He is fidgety. His right heel drums against the floor.

'In your cell?'

He nods again. Solemn. Like a child.

'Can I have one?'

He shakes his head. Slowly, and with intense focus, he folds the drawings into neat squares and slides them under his buttocks, like a child hiding his food. Then he raises his hands in mock surprise. 'Gone,' he says.

The warders at the door look at one another. They smirk, and I am overcome by an atavistic impulse to spit in their faces.

It's almost noon when I get to Mt Godwin at the top of the pass. The little town is a row of old veranda fronts with hanging baskets of pansies and ragged succulents. I am hungry, and I park outside the bakery.

Behind the counter a young girl is sliding a tray of custard tarts into the glass cabinet. She is small and slight, and her short hair is dyed a deep chemical red and cut in asymmetrical wisps. I ask for a sandwich and a custard tart and watch as the girl arranges them neatly in two small cardboard trays, then slips each tray into a white paper bag and folds the edges of the paper bags into a tight roll so that the contents will not fall out in the car.

'Are you Lexie?'

'Yeah.'

That slut is useless. 'Your aunt Lynnie says you're looking for work.'

The girl blushes and glances behind her to see if anyone is listening. 'Yeah.'

I turn my docket over and write my phone number on the back. 'I'm Erica Marsden. I live next door to Lynnie. If you're interested in doing some housework, or maybe a bit of gardening, you can give me a ring.'

Lexie looks startled. 'Thanks,' she says, almost in a whisper. She glances down at the docket. 'Thanks.'

That night, prowling the headland, I stop and sit on a flat rock above the blowhole. The sea is calm, like a vast pool of shallow water. There is a full moon and the long silvery flare of light on the water flows towards the horizon like the wake of a ship. On the horizon a boat is lit up like a floating carnival. And then I hear it, a loud sobbing, an aching wail that rises above the soft wash of the surf. It's only a short pathway through boobialla and wind-blasted she-oaks to where the sound is coming from, a house with all its lights on, though it's after midnight, and I walk towards it, careful to avoid the bandicoot holes that pockmark the thick spongy grass of the headland. I cannot see over the fence but I can hear the voices. A hysterical woman is crying and pleading: 'My phone—give me back my phone. I can't get home without it.'

'Too bad, you stupid bitch.'

A long wail. 'Give me back my phone. Give it back, please.' And then a scream. 'Get off me. Help—somebody help me!'

The male voice: 'I'll teach you a lesson.'

And then another male voice, calmer. 'Not while I'm here.'

'I need my phone. I need to ring my brother.'

'Stupid cunt.'

Another scream, and the second male voice. '*Whoa!* Not while I'm here.'

A woman in a bathrobe emerges from the house next door and strides across to the fence, which she thumps with her fist. 'Shut the fuck up, you lot, or I'll call the police.'

And suddenly it's quiet. A screen door bangs and the voices, muted, move inside.

I recognise this woman. It's the woman from the Duncans' party, the woman with the red kayak. Diana. And as if suddenly aware of my presence, she turns and says: 'Who is it? Oh, it's you.' Now, in the porch light, I can see that she is barefoot and wears a bright red silk kimono embossed with green birds. I nod in the direction of the fence. 'Are they always like this?'

'Only when they have a party.'

'How often do they party?'

'Too often.'

'Have you ever called the police?'

'No point. They're too far away. Anyway, they're not afraid of the police; they're afraid of me. I told them I'd torch their surfboards if they give me any more grief. They think I'm a mad old witch.' She beckons. 'Come in. We might as well have a nightcap.'

There is a big Mercedes van parked flush in the middle of the driveway and I have to walk around it. Diana has left the back door open and is in the kitchen, mixing us both a drink. Her kitchen is unrenovated seventies with an orange Formica bench and the living room is a bare glass box, sparsely furnished, that looks out to the

82

silhouetted rocks of the blowhole.

She hands me a tumbler of brandy. 'Sit down, Erica. Christ, you're thin. Do you want something to eat? Cooking's not my thing but I can get you some biscuits and cheese.'

'Thanks, but I'm fine.'

'So, what made you come to Garra Nalla?'

So direct. 'I wanted somewhere quiet to retire.'

'Well, it's certainly quiet. Except for the clowns next door.'

'You sound as if you don't care for the place.'

She shrugs. 'My husband's business went bankrupt and then my uncle died and left me this place. No kids of his own.' She sinks into a black leather couch and leans forward with her knees apart, elbows resting on her thighs, like a man. 'I saw you walking in the garden with Lewis Eames.'

'I asked for his advice.' The brandy burns my throat.

'On gardening? Lewis couldn't grow gorse.'

'I'm not interested in a garden.'

'Why not? It's so scrawny where you are, so…'

'Low-rent?'

'You said it, not me.'

'It's too sandy, not to mention salty and dry.'

'Why ask Lewis?'

'I'm thinking of building a labyrinth.'

'What on earth for?'

'I need a project. And they don't cost much.' I sound

83

vapid, but what am I to say to a stranger? 'I had this dream once, and…' And what? The words are not available to me, only the doing, and the making, if I can find a way. I turn to look out the window, to the flare on the horizon. 'Look at that. What is it?'

Diana leans back into the couch. 'It's a squid boat. The big attractor lights draw the squid to the surface. Tourists get all excited, they think they're seeing a UFO. They ring the police, who string them along and say, no, we don't know what it is.' She snorts her derision and raises her glass. 'Another?'

I am drawn to this woman. In her presence something in me is released. Her stark living room, suspended above the water, is like a room in one of my dreams, minus the radiant light. It has a monk-like austerity, as if the woman who inhabits it has never been domesticated, has never been encumbered with the petty and the trivial. I set my glass down on the coffee table and perch on the edge of an armchair. 'Have you lived here long?'

'Two years. My husband wanted to retire here and fish. Then he died. Got swept off the rocks.'

'I'm sorry. '

'So am I. I miss him. I miss having a sex life.' She points to the half-empty bookcase on the other side of the room. 'That's Max over there.' Diana, I realise, is drunk, drunk in the way of a seasoned drinker with only the least giveaway, a certain looseness of gesture, a propensity to sigh. On the top shelf of the bookcase is a photograph of a man in his late fifties, or perhaps early sixties. It's hard to tell because he is dressed in a kind of boilersuit and standing next to what looks like a rally car painted garishly in stripes and numbers.

'That's Max. Max and I used to drive in rallies. I was his navigator, but I was the better driver, not that Max would ever admit that.'

'Is that your van outside?'

'Bought that from the local plumber. Handles beautifully. And I wanted something I could sleep in. After Max died I took off for a while, drove around, slept in the back of the van. Then I got sick of cartons of long-life milk, and peeing in the bush. But what about you? What brought you here, Erica? Do you work?'

'I've retired. Early.'

'You don't give much away, do you?'

'What about you?'

'Do I give much away?'

'No, do you work?'

'I poison trees.' She laughs, a laugh that's almost a bark, and throws a muscular arm along the back of the couch. 'I work with Tom Robilliard. He lives just along from you on the other side of the Gittuses but I suppose you haven't run into him. You keep to yourself, don't you?'

'I haven't been here long.'

'No, well, Tom's a bit of a hippie. Lives off the smell of an oily rag but got a big grant to restore the forests around here, the ones that have been clear-felled and burnt. He

85

runs a team, including me. We cut the plantation pines and paint the blunt ends with herbicide. The pines die and the old forest regenerates.'

'Sounds like hard work.'

'It is. I come home buggered. Blisters on my hands and my nails are a wreck. I'm the only woman and I'm working alongside hoons on community work orders. It's *fuck this* and *fuck that*, and I'm twice their age and they don't know what to make of me. But at least I'm not sitting on my fat arse all day. Anyway, that's me. What about you?'

Now, having stayed, I must offer something. I tell her I used to manage a private hotel in the city, down by the quay, but that it has since been demolished and replaced by an apartment tower.

'Kids?'

'A son. He lives in the States.' This is an awkward lie. She deserves better. But I sense that her curiosity is half-hearted, that her interest in the past, even her own, is minimal.

'I see you at the beach, Erica, but hardly ever in the water.'

'I'm not a strong swimmer. And the lagoon can be a bit murky.'

'There's the sea.'

'Lynnie Gittus told me about the rip off the beach. I gather people have drowned.'

'Tourists. Some people get a false sense of security

when they leave home. You see them on the beach, jumping into the surf. Haven't a clue.'

'My breaststroke isn't up to a big swell.'

'Breaststroke?' She snorts again. 'I saw you breast-stroking in the lagoon the other day. You looked like a drowning possum. Come down in the morning and I'll give you a lesson in the crawl. It's all in the breathing. You'll soon get the hang of it.'

'That's very kind, but—'

Diana isn't listening, is gazing into her empty glass. Cloud has drifted across the moon and the light in the room has changed. She looks up, as if emerging from a trance, and in a half-distracted way reaches for the remote control and waves it in my direction. 'I was about to watch a movie,' she says, 'before that lot next door started up their racket. Interested?'

'It's a bit late for me, but thanks.'

'Well, come by anytime you're in the mood.'

She rises, and walks me to the back door. As we pass through her laundry she stops and points to a pair of padded gardening gloves lying in the sink. 'My planta-tion gloves,' she says. 'A new pair and already torn.'

'I thought you used secateurs.'

'Some of the time. The little ones you can pull out by hand but often you have to dig out the seedlings. It's killer work. I'll take you one day and show you.' She follows me out onto the concrete drive and stands in the moon-light with her arms folded, so solid a fixture, so imposing a presence, like one of those stone dragons at the entrance to a temple.

Out on the dusty road I turn to look back. The lights in the houses are out but I can see the flickering glow of a television screen in Diana's corner window. This is my hallucinatory world: the jutting headland in moonlight, the ghostly palaces of glass perched above the rocky shore, the lights of the squid boat ablaze on the horizon.

○

On Tuesday, promptly at 3.20, the girl Lexie ambles up the drive in her slow, absent-minded gait. She is dressed in what passes for the local school uniform: navy trackpants and a navy sweater embroidered with the school logo: *We Strive*. It's cool, and she wears a grey hoodie that's too small for her and frayed at the edges. She had rung on the Friday and we had discussed how she would get to Garra Nalla. She had offered to catch the school bus that delivers the children of the hamlet at the turn-off to the highway. But there was the question of how she would get home, back up the mountain pass, and I had offered to drive her. I asked Lexie to nominate an hourly rate and there had been a silence on the other end of the phone. And finally: 'Up to you,' she said. We had agreed on the rate she was paid at the bakery.

When Lexie gets to the front door she looks across to the dunes and says: 'There was an old guy who used to live here. He used to hide in the sandhills and spy on us.'

She pulls at the sleeves of her hoodie to cover her tattooed hands. 'We pelted him once with Coke cans.' She glances across the empty block of ferns to her uncle's house, where the veranda is empty. Ray hasn't been out there for days.

'Have you seen your aunt and uncle lately?'

The girl shrugs. 'Uncle Ray's in bed. Mum says he can't use his legs. Dad says his mind's bent.' She delivers these verdicts in a toneless voice of indifference.

I ask Lexie if she is hungry or would like a drink and she says no. Is she interested in gardening? She says she knows how to weed. Well, then, she can begin by weeding the overgrown rockery in front of the house. I give her an apron and some gardening gloves and lead her to the spiky rockery. 'Don't worry if you happen to damage any of the plants,' I say, 'because I don't like any of these cacti. I just can't decide what to do here, but meanwhile I'd like it to look like less of a jungle.'

After a while I glance out the window and see her leaning against the shed door with a half-smoked cigarette in her hand. And as I look on, she rolls up her left sleeve, extends her bare arm and jabs herself with the glowing butt. Even at this distance I can see that the skin on her arm is a livid network of scars.

I wait until Lexie has thrown the butt away and then open the door and call her in.

Late in the afternoon we climb into the car. At the bottom of the mountain pass the farm workers are out, spraying the crop with insecticide from a tank on the rear of a tractor. It seems that the long rows of small green plants, until recently a bare geometry of furrows, have grown and blossomed almost overnight: the vast paddock is a swathe of pale mauve flowers, their bright yellow stamens coated in pollen. 'Do you know what they've planted?' I ask.

'Potatoes.'

'I thought so.'

We are driving up the pass now, stuck behind a log truck, and the conversation is stilted. 'Lynnie told me they've just built a dam there, for the big pivot.'

'Yeah. Dad said it cost a million dollars.'

Lynnie had also told me that Ray had predicted disaster. They've put that dam in the wrong place, Lynnie had said one morning when we had been chatting beside the verge. 'Ray says there'll be trouble. One big rain and it'll overflow and we'll all be flooded.'

At the top of the pass the girl sighs. 'You're lucky to live by the beach,' she says.

'Come down anytime you like for a swim. You can always shower and change at my place.'

'Thanks.'

We turn off up a steep unsealed road where the rocky summit of Mt Godwin looms above us, a dense grey-green haze of old-growth forest. On the lower reaches a few houses lie half-concealed in bushland and Lexie points to a dark green wooden bungalow down in a gully at the bottom of a steep dirt drive. There is no gate across the drive, only gateposts on either side and on one of these is a big wooden angel fixed to the top. The statue must be at least five feet tall and has been hand-carved and varnished with a tawny resin. Lexie looks at me and says: 'My dad did that.'

'He's a wood carver?'

'He works for the council. Carving's his hobby, especially angels.'

It's now almost dark and the bush rears up behind the house. On its eastern side is a dry creek bed and above it a bank of prickly gorse. At the side of the house an old bus is parked, stripped of its tyres. A small boy is hanging out of an open window and staring up at the car.

'Your brother?'

'Jesse. He sleeps in the bus.'

'How old is Jesse?'

'He's six.'

Lexie gets out of the car. 'Thanks,' she says, and plunges down the steep bank towards the house. On the veranda a ginger mutt is lazing on a couch of tan vinyl, its cushions ripped and torn, the stuffing spilling out in a wild cotton froth.

Late in the afternoon I am joined on the terrace by Diana, who often turns up now for a pre-dinner drink. Since that night on the headland when we shared one of her stiff brandies she has assumed an intimacy based on nothing other than instinct, and a wordless understanding that seems, in retrospect, to have been there between us from the beginning. Not long after our first encounter beside the lagoon we had met up again at the turning circle and she had walked back along the road with me, taking my arm in hers, a gesture that had surprised and pleased me.

'You should have gone out and given her a slap,' she says, when told about Lexie's cigarette burn.

'Don't be ridiculous.'

'I would have done.'

'Yes, you would have done, and then she wouldn't come back.'

'Don't bet on it. Girls around here are used to being pushed around. And you're paying her.'

'What future is there for her in this place? She's saving up to go to the city when she finishes school this year.'

'Where she won't be able to afford to rent.'

'That'll depend on what kind of work she can get.'

'What will she do there?'

'I haven't asked.'

○

On the second Tuesday Lexie brings the boy with her. 'Sorry,' she says, 'I have to babysit.' Though Lexie is fair with delicate white skin, Jesse has olive skin and loose black curls. He has a cold and his voice is hoarse. He wanders around the house sniffling while his nose runs in a column of milky snot. Lexie produces a tissue from her sleeve and swipes at his nose with a rough intimacy.

The rockeries have been weeded and now, in their neatness, look even uglier. I lead Lexie to the back room, still crammed with cartons of books, so many there is space for nothing else. Here they sit in their boxes like ingots of lead, waiting for their dispatch into the smelter. But already I have run out of ideas for work that Lexie might do and all I can think of is to ask her to order and shelve Daniel's books. Of course there aren't enough shelves, but Lexie can at least organise them in alphabetical order and stack the piles against the walls, and, if necessary, along the hallway, and since she is a slow worker this should keep her occupied while I contemplate other options. Until then I am prepared to call a halt to my private auto-da-fé in the wood stove, confident in the knowledge that Lexie will show no interest in any of the books and will not ask questions, or want to borrow one, or make any observations as to Daniel's taste or reading habits. And Daniel will be none the wiser.

I suggest that Lexie carry the smaller cartons into the living room and then spread the books out on the floor with the aim of stacking them against the walls in columns. I Blu-Tack sheets of paper to the walls, each marked with a letter of the alphabet. It will be easiest for Lexie to go by author; to group them by category would be more complicated and she would have to ask too many questions.

The girl is quiet, but Jesse is a forward child who picks up anything he sees and looks at its bottom as if he expects to find something of interest there. He announces that he's hungry and I offer him some biscuits and cheese. 'Have you got any chips?' he asks.

'I'm afraid not,' I say, making a mental note to buy some and hoping Lexie will bring him again.

Later, as we walk down the drive to my car, Lexie and Jesse behind me, I hear the boy pipe up in his throaty old man's voice. 'Why does that lady live in a library?'

'Shh,' says Lexie. 'She'll hear you.'

○

All through this, the labyrinth is just an idea. And I am marking time in a suffocating present.

○

One morning I return from my walk to find three young men lazing on the terrace, their bicycles propped near the door. As I approach they rise and one of them steps forward to greet me. It's Indujan, my nephew, dark-skinned and dark-eyed (my brother's wife is Tamil). His blue-black hair is wound in a small knot at the base of his neck and his skin is glazed with sweat from riding in the heat. He shines.

I embrace him and he greets me formally in the earnest way of speaking that he's had since he was a boy. 'Hello, Aunty, I hope you are well.' He apologises for not phoning and says he and his friends have been on a cycling tour along the coast and have called in to say hello. He introduces the young men as Jamie and Aidan: they are

94

tall, blond and bronzed, as fair as Indujan is dark. Young gods, their teeth white and perfect, their eyes glazed with fatigue, as if they are stoned by the sun.

I guess that my brother has sent Indujan to check on me; he knows I am fond of the boy and would not turn him away. I offer the young men a cold drink and they remove their sandy shoes and enter the house. Once indoors I offer them a bed for the night and they readily accept. Indujan looks relieved. 'That would be great, Aunty, if it's convenient. It's very nice here, Aunty,' he adds. And then, 'Oh.' He has spotted Daniel's old telescope in the corner of the sunroom. It's a moment when he might enquire after his cousin but instead he asks if he can take the telescope outside and set it up on the dry sandy lawn. 'You don't mind, Aunty?'

'Of course not.'

Over dinner, Jamie tells me he has just spent three weeks in Mexico. He reaches into the small rucksack by his chair and pulls out a sketchbook, which he opens onto the table. I set my plate aside and begin to leaf through the pages, each with a single drawing of an intricately detailed mask or ceremonial headdress featuring a snake or a bird.

'These are very good, Jamie.'

'Would you like one?' He is so natural, so entirely without affectation.

'Are you an artist, Jamie? Is this what you want to do?'

'It was,' he says, 'but then I decided I wanted to be useful, so I'm training as a psychiatric nurse.'

I gaze at him in amazement. 'And where are you at with that?'

'I'm in my third year. Doing a placement at the Women's Hospital. In the anorexia unit.'

'He's learning to knit,' says Indujan, grinning.

'Wrong.' Jamie glares at him with mock scorn. And turning to me: 'It's crochet. The head of the unit thought the patients should learn to crochet, in a circle together'— with his left hand he traces a circle in the air—'and I'm learning with them.'

I find this startling, not least because it sounds like my father. *Put the hands to work and the hands will pacify the demons in the brain.* I could tell Jamie that Plato would have approved his decision, that he had banished artists from his republic because their imperfect imitations of the real offered only the emollient of meretricious charm, of false consolation, and hence were a distraction from the truth. But for *techne*, for the artisan who made things, there was an honourable role. Even for crochet.

Indujan is on his feet and clearing the plates from the table. 'C'mon,' he says, 'I've set up the telescope. We'll wash up later, Aunty, if that's all right.' He beckons us out onto the warm sandy grass where the evening star burns above the horizon. There we take it in turns to squint one-eyed into Daniel's telescope, to see the bright orb of Jupiter and its four specks of moons. Indujan points to the hills and names the red super-giant star, Betelgeuse. He tells us that the star on our side of the Southern Cross is the star closest to the Earth, only four light years away. The southern hemisphere is important to astronomers because the Earth is oriented in such a way that the southern hemisphere has less atmospheric distortion on the horizon and as antipodeans we get to see more of the inside of the galaxy. It's an idea that pleases him.

The night chill descends over the dunes and I offer them a nightcap. Wearily they accept before loping down the hallway to shower. When they have gone to bed I plug a silver foil of mosquito repellent into the power-point in the hallway and turn off the lights. At the end of the driveway loud heavy-metal music starts up with a thumping bassline but dies after only ten minutes.

We sleep.

And I dream that I am expecting a visitor and I must dress to welcome him, but when I open my wardrobe I find I have nothing to wear. I slide hanger after hanger along the metal rod but every dress is damaged: the fabric has been torn from top to bottom, the stitching of a seam has unravelled, a thread has pulled, the shoulders have been scorched by an iron or singed by a house fire. With a tug of increasing panic I fling the hangers along the rod but there is nothing intact and yet, behind my ragged garments, there is a row of Daniel's boyhood clothes, freshly washed and ironed and waiting to be worn. I must give them to the young men, I think. They will be needing something to wear.

We rise early. It's just after eight when I farewell Jamie and Aidan at the end of the drive but Indujan must return to the city by train, and will stay behind for lunch and take a swim in the lagoon.

In the late morning he bursts into the kitchen, wet, with patches of sand on his skin. 'There's a big stingray in the channel,' he says. 'I was wading across the mouth where it's shallow and I almost trod on it. It was huge.' He beams at me, alive with the wonder of it.

We eat out on the terrace. Indujan takes out his phone and says he has some photographs to show me from Parkes, where he has just spent two weeks working on his doctorate in astrophysics. 'Boy, was it hot out there.' He is keen to talk about his research, about high-mass stars born in dark and dusty environments where visible light can't penetrate but radio light can. I listen with a growing sense of the uncanny likeness that Indujan bears to my father: despite his exotic appearance and the blue-black knot of hair against the nape of his neck, it is Ken whom he most resembles. Already his manner of speaking is professorial, with a tendency to overuse the word *precisely* and to emphasise a point by spreading his fine-boned hands as if pressing down on the air. Indujan is Ken's natural heir, just as Daniel is the image of my wayward mother.

When I return to the terrace with coffee Indujan has

sagged in his chair. He is nervous and ill at ease. 'Have you seen Daniel lately, Aunty?'

It has taken him all this time to ask. He has waited until the last minute and forced the words out, because his father will interrogate him and he knows he must give an answer.

'Yes,' I say, 'I visit him every second week.'

'And he's well?'

The studied courtesy of this question is almost offensive. 'As well as can be expected.' Indujan might be clever but I suspect he is still a virgin, a kind of holy child who doesn't yet know what it's like to drown in the madness of sex, to have that snake writhe in your entrails until you can no longer bear it and lash out.

'Is he able to do his painting in prison?'

'It took a while but he's now been allowed some oil pastels. He draws. He can't have a paintbrush because he might use it as a weapon.'

'I see. And what does he draw?'

'He says he is a realist, that he will only draw what life there is in his cell. A spider, a fly, a scorpion. He draws them in great detail.'

'I see,' he says again.

I look down to where a column of ants is moving steadily across the cracked concrete. With great deliberation I set my cup back on its saucer but my hand trembles. 'Go, Indy, and pack your rucksack.'

We load his bike into the back of my wagon and drive

to Brockwood to catch the train. I lead him down to the old pier where the water is clear, blue, perfect. I show him the remains of the colonial whaling station, its handsome stone walls, the slab of granite where they hung the whales on giant hooks, and the great iron pot set into concrete where they boiled the blubber. Indujan is subdued. I thought he might mention his father; he has not. It's as if he knows he has been sent to negotiate some kind of entente cordiale and has failed, has not had the means or the maturity to pull it off. But he doesn't have to wait long for the train to rescue him. Within minutes it rattles to a halt across the road, and he turns to kiss me on the cheek, and then, with awkward haste, wheels his bike towards the platform, jogging and waving as he goes.

And I stand there, waving back. 'Give my love to your father,' I might have said. The words were on my lips but did not escape them. There was a great deal I might have said. I could have told him that one of the warders had asked Daniel for a portrait, and Daniel had readily assented, and the warder had sat for an hour, at the end of which Daniel had presented him with a finely detailed drawing of a cockroach. And had been bashed for his insolence. When last I saw Daniel he was a mess, his eyes blackened and swollen shut so that he could barely see and had to be guided to the table. His nose was strapped and bandaged in a way that told me it had been broken. He was unable to close his mouth and saliva leaked from one corner. But I had waited, impassive, waited until the warder stepped back. Then I took Daniel's hand and he winced, but did not remove it. And we sat for almost the entire session in silence and it was as if I were holding the hand of a mummy. But before it was time for me to leave he took a folded piece of paper from his pocket, and with a furtive glance from beneath lowered brows, pushed it across the table towards me. It was a drawing he had done some days before, the day after he had been bashed; he had opened his wounds and in his own blood had sketched the thick smudgy outline of a bogong moth.

Carefully, with the minimum of movement, I had taken the sheet and placed it on my knee. 'Thank you, Daniel,' I said. Then he gave his old crooked smile and, leaning across the table, whispered hoarsely into my ear: 'See, I have power here.'

With the sound of the train receding in the distance, I return to the car and rest my head against the hot sticky steering wheel. Time passes, the time that is without measure because there is nowhere to go, nowhere to be. I am flushed and a trickle of sweat runs between my breasts. The skin in the crevice begins to itch and it rouses me. I get out of the car and walk down to the whaling station. There I sit on the crumbling stone wall that looks out to a rocky island, half-covered in white seagull shit so that it resembles a layer of icing on a giant mound of damper.

Around seven I return to the car and drive back to Garra Nalla to park by the lagoon. Using my phone to light the path I walk down to its rocky edge where, balancing precariously on a large wet stone, I strip off, then turn to look for a marker among the shadowy cluster of tea-trees so that I will remember where I left my clothes. Wading into the water until it's up to my breasts I brush away the leafy seaweed that clings to my skin in slimy strands. Soon the dark maw of the water is enclosing me and as I dive below the surface I think of the stingray, its flat dun-coloured body merged with the grey sand on the floor of the lagoon. And as I begin my slow crawl towards the lagoon's deepest point I think of how easy it would be to turn towards the mouth of the channel, to leave this warm turbid water behind and swim out into the cleansing surf of the ocean. Instead, I swim on past the lagoon's deepest point, towards its far corner, until I arrive at the marshes. There I begin a steady breaststroke around the water's edge, close in to the shadowy clumps of sedge where the swans breed. I am not yet up to Diana's crawl, unable to sustain the rhythm of it, unwilling to immerse my nose and eyes. In the dark I have an image of my head moving across the surface of the water like a floating sphere, a silver bauble lit from within, and then the image fades, until with each thrust of my arms I feel the steady beat of a pulse beneath me, neither my own heartbeat nor the movement of the tide but something else, something both familiar and impersonal, something that almost against my will is keeping me afloat.

○

Of late I have abandoned the tacked-on little sunroom that at night is hot and stuffy, and now I leave my laptop and papers at one end of the kitchen table.

In mediaeval times the labyrinth was a feature of the great cathedrals where it became an emblem of Jerusalem, a pilgrimage site in miniature so that the monks traversed it on their knees. The most celebrated of these is at Chartres, a perfect circle with a rose at the centre. But I am not drawn to this pattern: too clerical, too rigid and symmetrical, lacking an organic feel, like a corset or an exquisitely designed straitjacket. The seed pattern has a roughness, an asymmetry that is not unlike the female breast. But Chartres is the more admired, and the complexity of its design is considered to be the most conducive to a state of mind where clock time has no meaning, and the impatient *I* is compelled to submit to the meander and its deferment of the goal.

There is another pattern, more like the seed, and conceived of as a form that could be used by both men and women in a situation of extremity. The Chakra-Vyuha features in the Hindu epic the *Mahabharata* as a fighting formation for infantry, a spiralling human fortress made up of armed bodies. But when inverted it becomes a yantra summoned by midwives to ease the passage of birth. The woman in labour must focus on the path as a way of relieving her pain and achieving the goal of a safe delivery…*the woman in labour is encouraged to visualize entering the Chakra-Vyuha and mentally treading the labyrinthine path in a state of deep absorption. In this way she enters into the field of her own womb in such a way as to summon up her mental powers to facilitate the birth.*

It all sounds so blithe. But my son did not come into the world as planned, and there was no treading the path. It was two days of agony in blood and shit and Gabriel Priest passing out while I went down, down like a miner into the bowels of some foul underground tunnel where this ruthless force within throttled my body until it surged into the open air on a wave of blood and ripped me apart.

'We'll call him Daniel,' his father said when he came to.

°

One day in the middle of dusting, Lexie stops and says: 'You have a lot of nice things.' This is a rare response to her environment. Sometimes she will study a picture on the wall, or a brass figurine. Today she is intrigued by the cast-iron firedogs below the mantel, a pair of armless Grecian statues with laurel wreaths on their heads, two robust male torsos that taper down into columns in the shape of a quiver of arrows.

'They belonged to my father.'

'Oh.'

And that is the extent of our conversation.

At the hardware store in Brockwood I had found a special implement for removing capeweed and bought it in the conviction that this will keep Lexie busy for a while and give her a break from arranging the books. The long rod must be stuck into the heart of the weed, one weed at a time, and the work is tedious. One afternoon I look out the window and see Lexie sitting on the grass beside the rod. She has removed her shoes and socks and is picking at her feet, peeling thin strips of calloused skin from her heels, and then the softer though still dry skin from the flat of her foot until she reaches the soft inner skin of the arch, where she draws blood. Then she stops, and taking a scrunched-up tissue from her pocket she dabs at the blood, pressing the tissue to the small wound to staunch the bleeding. After a while she holds it up to see how much blood has been shed and then shoves it up her sleeve. She puts her shoe back on, stands, and limping ever so slightly renews her thrusts into the capeweed.

What is it about teenage girls? Why must they inflict this self-torture?

When Jesse comes he talks nonstop and plies me with questions. He is a child who seems at home anywhere. One afternoon he arrives carrying a bag of vegetables sent by his father, a bag so full he has almost to drag it along the sandy drive. 'He wouldn't let me carry it,' says Lexie, half-apologetically. 'He always has to have his own way.' Jesse grins up at me. 'Dad grew this,' he says, as if the ownership were his and he is offering me a gift that puts us on equal terms, and I wonder where he got the confidence that his sister lacks. A bunch of curly purple kale, an iceberg lettuce with two healthy slugs nestling in its outer leaves, giant white leeks and a preposterously large head of broccoli like something out of a fairytale.

When Jesse doesn't come I find that I miss him. I say so to Lynnie, who grins. 'He's a cheerful little bugger. Had pneumonia last year and almost died. We were beside ourselves.'

I wonder if it were ever the case that Ray was beside himself, since he seems so utterly self-absorbed. I wonder too if Jesse is still sleeping in the bus. I had once asked Lexie if there was no room for him in the house. 'He could sleep with our older brother, Con,' she had said, 'but he doesn't want to. He loves the bus.' Wasn't it cold in winter? 'Jesse doesn't feel the cold,' Lexie had said. 'He's got his quilt. Mum made it for him.' No wonder he had pneumonia.

Occasionally Lexie surprises me. Today she pauses in the process of sorting books and brings one across to show me while I am chopping vegetables in the kitchen. 'Look,' she says. 'A picture of baby Jesus.' She smiles. 'He looks like Jesse.'

I dry my hands and take the book, open at a lurid illustration of the Messiah as a boy, and there is indeed a resemblance to Jesse, at least in the dark curls around his forehead. But what is arresting is the heavy underlining on the printed page opposite, and some illegible scribbling in Daniel's hand. Something here had meaning for him. I turn to the front of the book, to its title page, and it's one of Ken's books, an account of the apocryphal gospels.

'No need to sort this one,' I say. 'I'd like to look at it later.'

As soon as I return from driving Lexie home I go straight to the book and the pages that Daniel had marked. *At what age?* In the margins there are several asterisks, not the kind of mark a child makes. But at some point, it is clear, Daniel had read the *Infancy Gospel of Thomas*, and the heavily marked pages are an account of the occasion when the boy Jesus fashioned some birds out of clay on the Sabbath. When reprimanded for this by an old rabbi he breathed life into the clay birds so that they flew around the head of his interrogator. And Daniel had drawn small birds all down the margins of the page, tiny wrens with feathered fantails and tilted beaks. And at the bottom of the page he had scrawled: *Jesus was an artist*.

I turn the pages looking for further clues, and come to another story that has been heavily underlined, though this time there are no drawings. A child mocks the boy Jesus and throws a stone at him. Jesus curses the child and the boy's body withers and dies.

o

I receive a letter from my aunt Ruth, who asks that I come to the city and visit. 'I have something for you,' she writes. 'And I would like to see you.'

Is this a ploy by Axel to get me to meet with him?

After some days I ring Ruth. 'I'll come,' I say, 'but I don't want to see Axel.'

I hear her sigh. 'He's your brother and you're too hard on him. But don't worry, I'm not going to ambush you.'

Ruth has a curt way of speaking, a certain tone that conveys an old-fashioned quality of honour. 'Your aunt always does the right thing,' Ken had said once, though in relation to what I can't now recall. From England she had never failed to remember Daniel's birthday, and I remember a box of chalks and a book of hunting prints ('since you are interested in art'). Only after Ken's death had I discovered that Ruth had spent eight months squatting on Greenham Common with women protesting the installation of cruise missiles (by then her husband, Alf, was dead). For most of that time she had slept on a muddy field under a rough polythene shelter because the town council had banned tents. At night the local youths prowled around the women's settlement, jeering and throwing dog turds and bags of pigs' blood, and occasionally lit rolls of newspaper. It was reported that on one occasion hot pokers had been thrust through the polythene shelters on the perimeter. Some of the women mounted angry raids to break through the wire fence surrounding the missile silos and were rounded up by baton-wielding police. Many were imprisoned, but not Ruth. When Ruth had returned to live in Sydney and been asked about this episode by Axel she had given an account of it with a deadpan dryness that was hard to read. They had a lot of support, she said. Celebrities donated blankets and firewood. Paul McCartney sent a hamper.

Now Ruth lives on the aged pension in Blacktown. Her home is in a drab apartment block just off the freeway, opposite a newly built mosque.

I knock and Ruth opens the door, and gives me an appraising stare. 'You're very thin, Erica,' she says. 'I've made you a good tea.'

Though eighty-seven Ruth moves like a younger woman, briskly and with ease. From the rear you might think her a mere sixty. On her small round dining table, set with a white linen cloth, there are tea cups, a plate of sandwiches and a passionfruit sponge. On the stove a chicken casserole is simmering.

'Smells good.'

'It's the chorizo. And the vermouth.'

'How long have you been using chorizo?'

'Just because I'm old doesn't mean I live in the past. I go to the deli counter at the supermarket and I say: What's new? They're very helpful.'

In the evening Ruth sits up in bed reading second-hand recipe books that she buys from opportunity shops. A poor sleeper, she leaves the radio on all night, dozing between bulletins from the BBC World Service. 'Your aunt is very up on things,' Ken would say after he had rung his sister long distance. 'Gave me a lecture on the state of the Congo.' And he would mimic her clipped delivery from which all trace of an Australian accent had disappeared: 'How can anyone believe in a God, there or anywhere else?'

It's overcast outside, with black storm clouds massing in the west towards the mountains. On Ruth's tiny balcony, a kind of human bird's nest, are pots of herbs and a scarlet geranium in flower. She stands at the window and says: 'Look at those clouds. At my age you get a lot of pleasure from watching the weather. No two days are alike and it's all a bit of a mystery.' Then she moves across to the sink in her small fluorescent-lit kitchen, and fills the kettle. 'Get me the tea, dear,' she says, 'in the pantry cupboard behind you.'

I open the cupboard and it's astonishingly full, crammed with packets and tins and canisters and with a whole shelf of spices displayed in the biggest spice rack imaginable. There must be two dozen small tin canisters, neatly arrayed in a cedar rack with a carved kookaburra at either end. 'Where on earth did you get this?' I ask.

'It was your mother's.'

'Really? I don't remember seeing it.'

'Well, you were too young. It was *her* mother's and she didn't like her mother, or any of her family, and gave it to me. She didn't like to cook and she knew I did. And I want you to have it. I should have given it to you ages ago.' The mention of Irene is awkward and she wipes her hands fretfully on her apron. Ken had forbidden her to speak to me or to Axel about Irene and reluctantly she had agreed.

I am staring into the pantry, amazed at its plenitude. Old people are reputed to live on sausages and packet biscuits but here is my aunt with jars of artichokes and tins of smoked cod liver, and I want to laugh out loud. My ideal mother had always been there, freethinking *and* domesticated, but adjacent to my needs: not in the right place at the right time. Indeed, childless. I had once asked Ruth if she had wanted children and with characteristic economy she had replied: 'Alf couldn't have them and I wanted Alf.'

I reach for the tea canister and shut the door of the pantry. 'Thanks, Ruth, but I don't need a spice rack.'

Ruth tugs at the edges of the tablecloth in a show of straightening it, then cuts into the passionfruit sponge. 'I won't judge your mother. I never had children of my own, so I can't say.'

'Did you ever hear from her after she ran away?'

'No. I didn't expect to.' Her lips are pursed. She is holding her breath. 'You're looking tight, dear. Like you need a nerve day.'

'A nerve day?'

'Yes. When Alf was alive things would sometimes get very tense. I'd wait until the weekend'—Ruth had been a nurse—'and I'd have a nerve day. Wouldn't see anyone, wouldn't talk to anyone. Ate when I felt like it, slept when I felt like it and had a good read. Works wonders on the nerves.'

'You forget. I can do what I like now. I don't work and I live alone.'

'So you do.' Said with mild disapproval. Everyone

should keep busy.

'What's your news, Ruth?'

'I haven't got any news; I just wanted to see you.' She lays down her dainty cake fork. 'I don't think I've got long to go.'

'Have you had tests?'

'No. Just a feeling in my bones. But I do want to tell you this. You should see your brother. There's just the two of you now.'

'I saw Indujan last month. He came to visit.'

'So I hear.'

I wait for Ruth to remark that Indujan is a fine young man but my aunt is not a woman to state the obvious.

'Axel came to see me. He loves you, Erica. You're the only family he has.'

'He has his own family.'

'That's different. You were the nearest thing to a mother he had.'

'But I'm not his mother, Ruth. And we were never an ordinary family.'

'There are no ordinary families. And there's just the two of you now.'

'He never liked Daniel.'

'He loved Daniel. But he feared for him. He says he was a strange little boy. Obsessive. Always drawing.'

I will not go on with this. 'I've brought you something.' I reach down to my handbag, on the floor beside my chair. 'You sent me a picture once, of Ely Cathedral.

The chapel.'

'Good Lord, so I did. I couldn't get over it. It made quite an impression on me.'

'Me too.' I place the faded black and white postcard of defaced statues beside Ruth's plate and its half-eaten slice of passionfruit sponge. 'As you can see, I still have it.'

Ruth picks up the postcard and holds it at a distance, the better to focus without her glasses. 'Will you look at that?' Shaking her head. She takes a flower-print cotton handkerchief from her sleeve and dabs at her eyes. 'You've kept it all these years.'

'It meant a lot to me. It told me something when I was young but I didn't know what.' But I know now. It had consoled me; it had told me there was madness everywhere, not just at Melton Park, and that my mother absconding was not my fault.

I lift my fork and cut into the passionfruit sponge. 'This is good,' I say. 'I see you haven't lost your touch.'

Ruth is blinking back tears. 'There is far too much fuss about sugar these days,' she says. 'All things in moderation.'

The city, which once seemed dynamic and full of promise, now feels jaded and complacent—as if it has lost its sinews and become a mirage, a series of high-rise phantoms. But before leaving Garra Nalla I had decided that since I was going to be there I might as well walk the new labyrinth in Centennial Park. I will do this in the morning and then drive back to the coast. I have booked a room in the Corkhill, a hotel near Central Station with a dark foyer of black mirrored columns and black velvet wallpaper that is creepy and looks like a converted S&M parlour. I check in at the black Perspex reception desk but don't bother to take the lift to my room. Instead I stroll to Chinatown for an early meal. There, beside the giant stone dragons, I hear a voice call out to me. 'My God, Erica! It must be.' I turn, and a painfully thin man with greying hair is staring at me. It's Brian Murnane.

'Brian?'

'Yes. I wonder you recognise me.'

I am gazing at him in disbelief. 'You've lost so much weight.'

'*You* look just the same.'

We smile at one another in amiable surprise. But how gaunt he looks, how pale. He doesn't attempt to kiss me, or any other familiarity, and I am reminded that he always had a shyness about him which he didn't lose even when he drank, which was most of the time.

'What are you doing here? I heard you had moved to the coast.'

'Yes.' I don't say where, in case he might take it into his head to visit me. 'I'm here to see my aunt.'

'Are you here for long?'

'Just the night. At the Corkhill.' I nod in the direction of the hotel.

He hesitates, and I take him by the arm; through the

worn sleeve of his jacket I can feel the bone. 'I'm about to eat,' I say. 'Come with me. Or are you expected elsewhere?'

'No.' He shakes his head. 'That'd be good.'

We sit in the Golden Dragon, a cheap and noisy noodle joint popular with students, and he stares for a long time at the menu. This surprises me. Brian was never a fussy eater, indeed indifferent to food, as drinkers often are.

At last he looks up and says, 'I have to be careful—I'm diabetic.'

'Is this new?'

'They can't say. I nearly died. Kept losing weight, pissing all the time. Finally got a diagnosis.'

'Can you drink?'

'Not as much as before.' Which, I know, means he shouldn't drink at all.

'Where are you living?'

'In the old place.'

'What happened to Melbourne?'

'Rose didn't like it. So we came back.'

'How is Rose?'

'Dead. Breast cancer.'

'When?'

'Three years ago. She left me the house.' He shrugs his bony shoulders. 'Her nephews contested the will but…' His voice trails away. 'You should come and see the old place. I don't have many visitors. I'm a regular Miss Havisham.'

Alone, then, and with a failing pancreas.

He walks me back to the hotel. By the time we reach the automatic doors of the entrance I have made up my mind. 'Come in for a nightcap.'

'You sure?'

'Yes.'

We wait beside the lift and he looks around at the velvet wallpaper and the black glass columns and grimaces. 'It's like an S&M parlour,' he says. And I laugh. We always did think alike.

In the small, stuffy room on the ninth floor we lie together, side by side. Brian is a living skeleton and I am surprised he could manage an erection.

'You didn't come.'

I pat his bare chest where thin strands of charcoal and grey hair remain. 'Not possible.'

Brian seems to intuit my meaning: the slow-moving glacier of pain I live within renders me unable to lose myself in another, which would in any case feel like a betrayal. Though of whom, and of what?

For a while we lie in silence, and then Brian, in an almost whisper, says: 'Daniel was a beautiful boy.'

'Please.' I place my hand on his shoulder. 'Please,' I say again. 'Go home now.'

I watch him dress, his body an abject geometry of painful angles, his clothes hanging about his limbs like limp flags.

'I'm in the book,' he says.

I nod.

He opens the door and in the shadowy night light of the corridor raises his hand, palm outward. I raise mine, a mirror of his.

In the morning I am amazed to find I have slept well. I check out early and drive across town to Centennial Park. The park is vast and I must use my GPS to find the newly installed labyrinth, which is located at the northern end of Willow Pond. It's a warm, humid morning and the park is alive with joggers and the jangling bells of cyclists. There is a rich smell of damp grass, and of something indefinable like a blend of citrus and hops.

The labyrinth is set in a grassy clearing, a mandala of bleached paving in sandstone and bluestone, an exact copy of the one in Chartres Cathedral. And how bare it looks. Too perfect. I estimate that it must be around eighteen metres wide and I note the camber of the surface, presumably so the water will run off in the city's subtropical downpours. But that camber must have been difficult to install and I ponder the complexity of constructing its subtle curve, the expense of it, the many calculations it would have demanded, the exacting precision.

At the opening to the meander I hesitate and then begin to walk it, but almost at once the path seems too narrow, or is it that my ageing body is beginning to lose its balance? By the time I reach the centre I am certain that this complex mandala is not for me. Something is missing:

some quirk, some local *ingenia* of the improvised and unexpected. Am I being perverse? The Chartres works for others. It must do: it is there.

I don't bother to walk the path back to the opening but break the rules and cut across the lines to head for the adjacent patch of swampland and its seductive grove of paperbarks. The path there is wet and muddy underfoot, yet the paperbarks have an allure that the paved labyrinth has yet to acquire. The mud squelches beneath my shoes and I must take care not to slip on the sodden path, yet the paperbarks are alive and enfold me in their commonplace mystery. I am glad I came.

On the drive back to Garra Nalla I reflect on how stark the stone paving of the labyrinth appeared. How can I avoid this in my own construction? How can I create something that merges with the dunes—that suggests unity rather than separation? How can I bring nature and the made work into a right-seeming fit? In the city I had looked up at the celebrated new multistorey building on Broadway with its great wall of vegetation and recoiled; it seemed dishonest, and worse, it looked uncanny, like the beginning of a ruin.

It's just after nine when I arrive at the shack, and I go straight to the kitchen table to open my laptop and stare at the seed labyrinth that I have made into my screensaver. My thoughts come to me now in a rush, a kind of mental shorthand. I must find a way to begin soon. If I lapse into apathy I will lose the blessed sense of spaciousness that came to me in the dream in my apartment, the dream that had felt like a gift. Unearned and unbidden, it might never come again, and the gap, that sandy stretch of land outside my door with its parched little tufts of grass and weed, will remain just that: a windswept wasteland. All I do is sit and stare at my screen, unable to decide even on the form of the thing, unable to make a tentative beginning. Caught between the cramped interior of my grief and the wide, open plain of the dream, I am unfocussed and unarmed. Like my mother, I am impractical. I must find someone to build this labyrinth for me.

Part 2

the
labyrinth

It's warm and it's quiet. The blowflies can smell the chicken roasting in the oven and buzz manically around the screen door. I go outside to gather in the washing and stand at the old line strung between two weathered poles, and for a few moments am immersed in the vibrating hum of mid-afternoon.

The washing is stiff from sun and salt, and I carry it inside and spread it over the clotheshorse in one of the bedrooms, a room still stacked with cartons of unpacked books. As I walk back out into the hallway I hear a faint, high-pitched squeak, and then another. I look up and there clinging to the lintel is a small bat, its legs tucked above its cigar-shaped body, its soft brown fur encased in grey translucent wings. I walk to the laundry to look for a cloth bag, and think I might brush it into the bag with a short-handle broom.

When I return the bat is gone.

That night I see a small shadowy shape in flight beside the window, and wonder at a bird flying under the eaves at this hour. But then the dark shadow swoops across the room, diving and wheeling, and I see that it's the bat. I jump up from my chair and retreat like a startled animal to my bedroom. And shut the door. How to remove it? Could I throw a net over it? But I don't have a net. I ring Diana, who says to shut all the internal doors and open the others so it can find its way out. 'It won't come near you. Its radar will tell it you're an obstacle.' I put on a hat and a thick padded jacket from fear that the creature will rake my head or catch on my sleeve. Then I open the bedroom door. The bat is panicked, diving and swooping in asymmetric loops between living room and kitchen, and I fling open the back door and then, ducking my head, the front door. And retreat to the bedroom.

An hour passes and I open the bedroom door. There is no movement in the living room. Perhaps the bat has settled on a ledge and roosted for the night. Listen for the squeak, Diana had said. I listen, but hear nothing. I lock the doors.

In the morning Diana explains that bats are roosting in my roof at night. They enter through a gap in the eaves (haven't I noticed the smears of bat shit on the big side window?). One of them must have found a hole somewhere in the ceiling and become trapped in my living space. That afternoon I look carefully and methodically in every room but can find no point of entry. Which means it will probably happen again. I must buy a butterfly net, or something similar from the fishing counter at the hardware store. At night I can sit with the net beside me.

The next day I drive to Brockwood and enquire at the hardware store. Of course, they have no net. 'Haven't seen one of them for years,' says the old guy behind the counter. 'What's it for? Butterflies? You a collector? A leper…leper…'

'A lepidopterist.'

'Yeah, one of them.'

'Not exactly.'

Outside in the crystalline light I walk to the marina to buy fish off the boats, a fat fillet of stripy trumpeter. I will cook for Diana, who lives off tinned salmon and avocado and expensive packet soups from the deli that she eats with water crackers and chunks of strong cheddar. The marina is quiet: it's not yet the tourist season, when the gulls will clamour and swoop for every oily chip they can scrounge. Today they are merely watchful, idle on the bollards of the pier.

I drive on to the CO-OP, hoping there is bread left from the Saturday bake. In recent days a relaxed mood has come over me and I can perceive no reason for this other than that I live by the sea. Lynnie Gittus has read that the negative ions given off by ocean water have a tonic effect on the body's electromagnetic field, but Lynnie and Ray are susceptible to the belief that invisible forces can play havoc with their sanity and must perhaps conjure a coun-tervailing force in order to stay cheerful. Well, Lynnie at least is cheerful; Ray is a lost cause. This morning on my way out of town I had waved to him, as is my perverse custom now, and as usual he had looked away as if I were the Medusa with the evil eye.

It's a Monday, and quiet, and the only other customer in the CO-OP is a young man in frayed denim shorts and a worn T-shirt. We arrive at the checkout together, he ahead, and the girl at the register, Amy, who is always chatty, says: 'Hi, Mrs Marsden, do you know Yerko?'

'No, I don't.' I turn to him. 'Hi, Yerko.'

'Hello.' He nods, formally, and says in a thick accent, 'I am pleased to meet you.' And then, solemnly: 'It's Jurko, with a J, and not Yerko but Yewerko.'

Amy laughs. 'Well, excuse *me*.'

He grins. 'Is all right. A strange name for you.'

Jurko is very thin and his hair and beard are long and tangled. His skin is dark from the sun, but his features are fine and his pale blue eyes look back at me with a child-like stare.

'*Jewerko* is looking for work,' says Amy.

'Oh,' I say, 'and what kind of work do you do, Jurko?'

'I am a stonemason by training, but I do anything, anything you like. You tell me what you want, I do it.'

'Right. I'll keep that in mind.'

He pays for his few items: a packet of brown rice, a plastic container of miso paste and a bunch of spinach. He counts out some change, looks up, nods at me again, and at Amy, and walks out to where an old pushbike is propped against the wall.

'He's new around here,' offers Amy. 'He's camped out the back of Shelly Beach.'

'But that's a national park.'

'Depends. He might be just on this side of the border. That's where I'd camp, where the river runs out. It's flat, and sheltered.'

'He told you this?'

'Yeah, I asked him where he lives. If he wants work, people have to know where to find him. And he doesn't have a phone. Said he doesn't believe in them.'

'What's his other name?'

'Don't know.'

On the drive home, it comes to me: a stonemason. He would surely know how to lay a paved labyrinth, or construct a stone one. And if he is broke and camping in the wild he is unlikely to be expensive. On the other hand, he might not be reliable. It's almost five weeks and I have yet to hear from Lewis Eames, and when I do I know what the answer will be.

That night I am restless. I sit at my laptop and wonder if I really am ready to begin. It would be easy to remain in this fugue state of apathy, to have always an idea, a half-formed plan that never materialises. The material world is too intractable.

I get up from the table to lie on the cane sofa and doze for a while, reluctant to go to bed. And dream that I have just woken to find a small boy in my sunny kitchen. The boy is sitting cross-legged on the cork floor and nursing a coiled black snake that rests on his lap. Before I can utter a warning the boy begins to play with the snake, flipping its head and laughing as its tongue darts in and out of its black scaly jaws. I reach for the straw broom, propped in a corner, and flick the snake onto the floor where it elongates into a slithering curve. While the boy grins, I sweep the serpent to the back door, holding my breath and trusting that it won't make a sudden move to the side and down the hallway. But the door opens of its own accord so that in one fluid stroke I am able to loft the creature onto the cracked concrete outside. Within seconds it disappears into the tall cactus blades of the rockery.

I wake. It's still dark. I get up and wander into the kitchen, faintly disoriented, and switch on the light, half-expecting to see a reptile on the cork tiles. I glance at the clock on the oven and it's just after five. Now I am wide awake and will make tea and toast and sit at the table strewn with papers and shuffle yet again through images of labyrinths, and wait for the sun to rise up over the sea. I am waiting.

The weather is increasingly unpredictable and the late afternoon brings a sudden unseasonal hailstorm. White balls of ice cover the beach and the sparse yellow grass on my lawn. The assault is so heavy and prolonged that three Pacific gulls take shelter under the woody old geranium bushes at the rear of the house. When the storm subsides I climb over the sandhills to find dead penguins among piles of black seaweed dumped on the shore. I begin to prod and pick at the thick belts of rubbery kelp, looking for small sponges shaped like trees that occasionally wash up after a storm. Further up the beach I can see a big piece of driftwood on the wet sand and as I approach I am struck by its smooth dark surface, the way it glistens in the sun. But when I lean in for a closer look it rears up in fright, flapping its flippers and waddling back into the surf in a panicked retreat. A seal, cast up by the storm and dozing in the wake of the retreating tide.

o

It's Sunday, and I drive out to the northern border of the national park where the River Styx flows into the ocean. I have to clamber over boulders covered in orange lichen and it occurs to me that if I should slip and twist an ankle, or break a leg, no one will know I am here. And what does it matter if I fall on the rocks and hit my head? What do I care now; what do I have left to lose? And yet a muffled voice in my chest says, yes, yes, it does matter. It still matters. It matters to get to the end of the beach.

The beach is long and sloping and I walk close to the water, where the sand is firm. The cockleshells crunch underfoot and I am careful to avoid the spiky pufferfish stranded below the high tideline. I am carrying a light backpack because I have brought a walnut cake with me, in a tin, as a gesture of goodwill; had jammed it into the backpack before I left, a foolish idea since it has made my climb over the rocks all the more awkward. Why hadn't I just driven to the CO-OP and left a message with Amy?

But I am in luck; it's a mild day, overcast and with no wind, and I find Jurko sitting beside his tent where the river runs out in a trickle over smooth grey stones. The tent is visible from the other end of the beach and I am surprised that he has made no attempt to conceal his refuge. Perhaps he intends to camp only a short time, though I suspect he is an illegal immigrant who has overstayed his visa. Behind him a line of tea-tree rises high, but so spindly are their trunks that they could not possibly offer him protection from the wind.

Jurko is reading a book and when he sees me says, 'The woman in the supermarket, I think.'

'Erica Marsden.' I extend my hand and he leans over and shakes it with a loose, dry grip. His skin is leathery, his hand calloused. His long straggly beard is encrusted with salt. I try unobtrusively to see what he is reading but without my glasses am unable to tell. 'May I sit down?'

'Sure, sure.'

I sit cross-legged on the warm sand and its spiky tufts of grass that prick at my skin. 'You said in the supermarket, Jurko, that you are looking for work.'

'This is true.'

'Have you found any?'

'A little, yes. I do some days for a wood carter at Mt Godwin. I think I will do some more.'

Mt Godwin? He cycles up the steep mountain pass? 'I

was wondering if you would be interested in doing some work for me.'

He stares at me. 'What kind of work would this be?'

'I'm thinking of building a labyrinth.'

'And why do you want to do this?'

His question is so direct it takes me by surprise. I haven't prepared a mundane answer. 'I'm not entirely sure.'

'You don't *know*? Surely you have given this some thought.'

'It will be a garden feature, I suppose.' How lame this sounds but it will do for now. 'It's very sandy where I live. Too sandy to grow anything.' I would make a joke of it. 'I might as well grow stones.'

He shakes his head. 'I think you are a strange woman. I thought so the first time I meet you, in the supermarket.'

'Really?'

'Yes, you look angry. But you have two faces. The angry one and the other one.'

'I think that might be true for all of us,' I say, though I know it isn't. Two-faced is exactly what I am. 'If you're interested I'd like to discuss it with you.' I look around and gesture towards the bay. 'But not here.' The sun has come out from behind the clouds and is blinding me. 'Would you be interested in coming to my place to discuss it? I'd pay you for your time.' And then it occurs to me that he has only a pushbike and it's a long ride to Garra Nalla. 'I could pick you up from outside the supermarket and drop you back. We could have lunch.'

'Well,' he says, in his singsong English. 'It could be interesting.' And he shrugs. 'But I make no promises.'

How quaint this sounds, as if he is a prince and I a petitioner for his favours. 'Good. What about Wednesday, around ten?'

'Sure, sure.'

'Okay, good. See you then.' I wonder if I should linger for small talk. Have you been here long? How do you cook your food, since there is a permanent fire ban around here? But I would sound like I was prying, or worse, an older woman who prattles. I stand and brush the sand from my legs. 'Where are you from, Jurko?'

'I am sorry but this is none of your business.'

I nod. 'Right.'

But Jurko frowns, as if giving the question more thought. 'I don't tell you this—best you don't know.'

'Why?'

'If anybody ask you, you can give honest answer.'

'Why would I want to lie? If I knew, that is.'

'I think we don't talk about this anymore. I could make up a place and you would be none the wiser.' He shrugs, and holds his hands out as if to say: Don't persist, you foolish woman.

What began as a sea breeze has turned into a cold blustery wind. 'The wind's come up and I'd better get back,' I say.

'Yes, and I will be seeing you soon.' He, too, stands and gives a little bow, and I see that he is skin and bone, and that his cut-off jeans are held up by an old leather belt pulled in tight. Then I remember the cake, and unzip the backpack to extricate the tin. 'I thought perhaps you might like a cake, since you have no oven here.'

He opens the tin and stares as if appraising a piece of stone that might or might not do. 'Cake is unhealthy,' he says. 'But it is good for you to do this.'

I think he means 'good of', but I can't be sure.

o

Lexie is sitting cross-legged on the floor, unpacking yet another carton. All around the living room there are piles of books stacked against the walls. Lexie is slow but she is neat and at times she will hover intently over a growing column of books to adjust the balance so that the column doesn't topple.

Lately I have been giving some thought to what Lexie can do next and this morning it occurred to me that the wood on the window frames is badly stressed by sunlight and salt-laden wind; it's dry and splintering and Lexie might be employed to sand and varnish the external surfaces. So slow a worker is she that without the use of a sanding machine it's a task that could occupy her for months. But perhaps Lexie will soon find other work. When she arrived this afternoon I made my usual enquiry about how things were going and discovered that she is soon to enrol in a barista course run by the school. And what better way to get work in the big city for an unskilled country girl? 'Good,' I said, 'you can practise on my coffee machine. It's just a simple one but I'd like that. It's rare that anyone makes me a coffee.' Okay, she said, in that affectless way of hers, and I felt buoyed by the thought that we might have something to talk about down the track, since Lexie is resistant to any of my efforts at conversation, and it seems unlike ordinary shyness but the reserve of a mind engaged elsewhere. On some days she can appear almost robotic, except when Jesse is with her and then her affection for him is touching, her pride in him, as if he were not an annoying sibling but her own son. If it were not for the fact that Lynnie had said she was saving up to go to the city and find work there, I would by now have come to the conclusion that Lexie was one of those small-town girls who lives in a waking dream, marking time until she can become a mother.

°

Wednesday, 9.40, and I am early. But when I turn into the car park of the Brockwood CO-OP I see that Jurko is already there, waiting beside the automatic doors with a khaki backpack at his feet. I wind down the window and wave to him. 'Where is your bike?' I ask.

'We don't worry. Amy has found a safe place for it.' Evidently he is not so great a hermit that he is unable to make friends.

On the drive back to Garra Nalla I am nervous at first but it turns out that Jurko is quite a talker, with an opinion on most things. 'This coastline'—he gestures at the window—'it could be lovely but is degraded. There is no new industry here, no jobs, so why develop the land? All these little blocks pegged out, and for what?' And he lectures me on the unruly development taking place, which is a bit rich given that he is camping illegally in a national park.

We turn into my drive and Jurko looks around him and nods. 'This is a good spot, I think. It's good to be flat, though not essential.' When I unlock the door of the shack he strides past me into the living room, and then off down the hallway as if he has come to inspect the building. He is uninhibited in the way that some children are, and I have an uncomfortable feeling that he is indeed a kind of man-child with no proper sense of boundaries.

'I like your house,' he says. 'There has been very little waste in building this house, yuh? People have recycled.'

'That's one way of putting it. Other people call it a hodgepodge.'

'No, not hodgepodge.' He also has a way of making every statement sound like a definitive judgement, which doesn't in the least dispel my fear that he might be a little crazy.

'I'm glad you approve, Jurko.'

'Yuh, it's good.' If not crazy, he is certainly without irony. He looks around him and picks up my black flip-top phone from the farmhouse table. Another liberty. 'You don't have a smartphone,' he says, as if this surprises him.

'I used to have one.'

'This is interesting.'

'It is?'

'Yuh.' He nods, and frowns like I am missing the point.

'You'd like one?'

'Me? Phuh!' he snorts dismissively. 'Would I need this GPS, this satellite woman telling me where to go?'

Yes, perhaps it would make him easier to trace. 'Well, shall we have some coffee?'

He shakes his head. 'I don't drink.'

'Tea?'

'I take no caffeine. I drink only green.'

'Okay, green tea it is. Let's sit out on the terrace.' So disconcerting is his presence—striding down the hall, picking up the phone—that I feel more comfortable with the idea of Jurko outside the house rather than in. I make a pot of green tea and carry it out to the terrace, where Jurko is inspecting the grounds. When we are settled I venture an enquiry into his background. 'Where did you train as a stonemason, Jurko?'

He stares at me as if this is an impertinent question. 'I train from childhood. My father, my uncles, my grandfather, all are stone masters.'

'And where were they based?'

He is chewing on an oat biscuit and makes an odd coughing sound as if he has difficulty in swallowing. Solemnly he lays the biscuit down on his plate and says:

'All right, I tell you. My family are Albanian, but my mother Serbian. I was born in Podgorica but you won't know this place. Podgorica is the capital of Montenegro but we don't stay there for long. We travel everywhere, for work.' And he unzips the backpack he has brought with him and pulls out an embossed leather photo album. 'Look, I bring this to show you.' He turns the pages of the album and points to photographs of three different churches, some in long shot, others in detail. 'This is Kotor Cathedral, older than many cathedrals in Europe. Two years on this. Most of my apprenticeship, yuh?'

'This is Orthodox?'

'No, Catholic. But doesn't matter—all religions are the same.'

'You carry this book everywhere with you? It's so heavy.'

'Of course. If I want work, I must show myself.'

'You must have a great love of churches.'

'No, no love.' He says this rather too loudly, and with a strange rising inflection as if issuing a warning. He is staring at me, that stare again, and there is a look in his glacial blue eyes that I find unsettling. 'I tell you, religion is a business, just a business like anything else. They drive a hard bargain; they try and do you down. Do they love the poor? Of course not. This love of the poor is a joke.' He shakes his head. 'There are no beds in churches.'

I tell him the story Lynnie had told me of the one church built in Garra Nalla, a tiny Anglican chapel from the colonial era that for years had sat unsteadily on stone blocks until in the 1980s it blew over in a gale.

He gives a high-pitched, whinnying laugh. 'Good riddance, yuh?'

Slowly I turn the pages of the album but there is nothing in it of a personal nature that might be revealing. After I have handed it back to him I reach for the folder that lies on the table between us. Inside, on printed sheets, are nine labyrinth patterns. 'Here,' I say, handing him the loose collection of sheets. 'Do you have any opinion of these?'

Jurko studies them for a minute or two and looks up. 'Most of these are too complicated, I think.'

'Really? What would you suggest?'

'You must choose, of course, no one else.'

'What about this one?' I hold up the Chartres pattern, though I have not for a minute contemplated trying to emulate it.

'Chartres!' Jurko snorts through his beard. 'This is exactly what you don't want. Nothing like.'

'Too complicated?'

'Yes, definitely too complicated. But more relevant to the point, is too foreign. You Australians copy other peoples. Chartres this, Bali that. You should have your own world. Not copy.'

'Bali?'

'Yes, I think Australians love Bali.'

'I've never been.'

He shrugs. 'Nothing wrong with that place but good to make your own world.'

I am in my own world, Jurko, more than you know, and more than I ever wanted to be. 'You think I should look for a new design?'

'Yes. Maybe like a tree.' He points to the soft drooping she-oak on my boundary. 'Maybe like *that* tree.'

He can't be serious. The she-oak is thousands of fine filaments, impossible to reduce into even a stylised pattern. No, he is being contrary. I wait while he reaches for another biscuit, and notice for the first time that his nails are bitten to the quick.

'Have you been to Chartres?'

'Of course. I backpack there with friends. But we do not see the labyrinth, and in any case, it's no big deal. For some, maybe, but not for us. Most days it's covered with chairs so you can't see it. The priests want to control it, like everything else.'

I change the subject. What else has he built since he came to Australia?

'One thing only. I build a holiday house in Port Lachlan.' He stares out towards the dunes. 'Very bad experience for me. The husband own a chain of liquor shops; his wife has shops that sell women's underwear and bikini things. They say they want a house like a Balinese temple, with canvas sails.' He snorts. 'Bali this, Bali that. In the end they don't pay me; I get ripped off. I am treated like a dog. Every night I sleep on the beach and I think of how I might punish them. I think about this for a long time.' He turns towards me with his boyish smile. 'But then they die in a car crash.'

Yes, he's a nutter. I should give up on this. But then, as if someone else is speaking, I hear myself say, matter-of-factly: 'Oh. So you will never get your money. I'm sorry.'

'No. But I did not sin, either. So you see, God looks after me.'

'So you feel God directs you?'

He shakes his head. 'Not all the time, no. But when I need it, yes. This is the lesson I learn in Port Lachlan.'

'The lesson?'

'Yes. I lose my reason. But don't worry, now I have it back. I live here for a while, I camp by the river, I sleep on the earth and it comes back to me.'

I hesitate, and wonder how I can exit this situation without ill will. But when I open my mouth, again it's as if someone else is speaking. 'Well, after that story I think maybe I should pay you in advance.'

'Not necessary. You I trust.'

'Can I ask why?'

'Because I have seen your house. Your house tells me.'

Tells you what? I could ask, but am silent. His intensity is disturbing, but also compelling, as if unsullied by the banality of the everyday. His skeletal body, his ragged hair, his chapped lips are suggestive of something otherworldly, though I remain uncomfortable with the way he stands too close to me, as if he has no awareness of the polite boundaries of the body's physical space: his, mine or anyone's.

I stand, and begin to gather our plates and cups onto the tray, and say I have arranged to see a friend in the late afternoon and had better drive him back to Brockwood. We can meet again in a few days if he is free.

On the drive along the coast road Jurko is silent. He rests his head against the window and appears to fall asleep. Is he ill? Have I offended him? Does he sleep badly in his tent? When we arrive at the CO-OP I offer to wait while he collects his bicycle and drive him back to his campsite. No, he says, he would rather ride.

On the drive home, free of his unsettling presence, I feel a pang of something like guilt. There are no beds in churches, he had said, but there are empty rooms in my house and I hadn't offered him one. Of course not. He is a stranger, and he's odd, not because he's foreign but because he's just, well, odd. How do I know he won't rob me, or attack me in my sleep?

I eat supper in the kitchen and gaze at the papers strewn across the table. Surely it's no coincidence that I should meet up with an itinerant stonemason at precisely the moment when I have decided I must make a start on the labyrinth? But does this young artisan have to be so weird? I attract these people, I think. I always have.

Later I will walk up to Diana's for a drink on her deck and we will look out to the moon rising over the water and I will tell Diana about Jurko. 'He's either mad or some kind of holy fool,' I say.

'Holy what?'

'You know, innocent. A purist.'

'Honestly, Erica, you are so gullible. He's more likely schizophrenic and off his medication. Or he's outstayed his visa and he's hiding.'

○

After breakfast I set out for my daily walk along the beach, waving, as usual, to a sullen Ray on his veranda.

Once again I collect Jurko from outside the CO-OP. As I pull into the kerb he waves and breaks into a smile, which surprises me; I realise I haven't seen him smile before. Until now he has been earnest and hectoring. Could it be that he is pleased to see me?

It's a dull, overcast day with heavy cloud. The kitchen is dim and I turn on the lights. 'This is waste,' says Jurko. 'You can see already without these lights.'

'I like the lights on when it's dull. It's cheerful.'

'Yes, but a waste.'

'Let's look at the designs, shall we? I need to decide on a pattern and I have more designs I want to show you.' I have set up the kitchen table with books, and diagrams run off from the internet, and two blank notepads. I don't offer Jurko tea for fear of a further lecture on waste, and to distract him I show him the book of labyrinths installed in the London underground.

Jurko flicks at the pages, then sits back in his chair,

arms folded. He points at the page open in front of him, a sharp-edged geometric design with four quadrants in the Roman style. 'What use is this?' he says, 'if you can't walk it?' He waves at the book dismissively. 'Just for show.'

'I agree, but the book is a useful reference. So many designs.'

'Too many, I think.'

'Yes. But look, Jurko, they all have something in common. Two things.' I take a drawing of the seed labyrinth from the pile and place it between us. 'See.' And I begin to trace the pattern with my finger. 'First, there's the *meander*, which is the pathway. And it can't be simple; it has to double back on itself and have unexpected turns.'

'Not so unexpected, I think.'

'Well, in theory. And perhaps nothing worth having is straightforward.'

'The opposite, I think.'

'Well, we can debate that later.' I return to the drawing. 'So there's the *meander* and then there's the *spiral*, which is the overall pattern.' I look up at him. 'And isn't it interesting, Jurko, that the spiral is found in so many places, in the double helix of the DNA molecule, and the way the galaxy spins?'

'Yuh, this is true. So what?'

'Well, the spiral is supposed to represent nature, but the meander is man-made. Man and nature come together in a harmonious pattern. That's the idea, at least.'

Jurko is looking at me intently. 'You read this in a book?'

'Yes. But I am capable, Jurko, of having my own thoughts.' I say this with a touch of irritation and lean back in my chair. 'Would you like some tea?'

'Yes, please. And a sandwich, if you have.'

'Of course.'

Over the next hour I show him a selection of simple single-path patterns, rounded in form, but also some of the square ones used in Roman designs, and I explain why I dislike the latter because to my eye they appear harsh and geometric: too many straight lines and sharp angles. And always with a Minotaur at the centre, a force which the Romans, typically, thought they could subdue, as they subdued all else. But even the rounded patterns can look like a straitjacket, forms that spiral into the centre like a bull's eye because all the paths are concentric and thus there is no cross in the pattern and hence no crossover in the middle. The effect is hypnotic and over-focussed because there is not enough meander. Too masculine, I might have said if I had been describing it to Diana. But Jurko is in agreement. 'I don't like this,' he says. 'It shouts at you, yuh?'

'It does.' And I wonder how long he has been in the country, for his English is really very good, even his use of the vernacular.

He grins. 'Another sandwich would be good. And toasted. Hot food is best, better for the digestion.'

'I hope you're not skipping meals, Jurko.'

He stares at the page in front of him. 'Sometimes,' he says enigmatically, and I wonder if he has run out of money.

I remember that I baked some biscuits for him the day before, burnt butter with a sliver of ginger on top, which is odd since I am not a biscuit-making woman. Why this impulse to bake? Because Jurko is freakish and might somehow be contained by the domestic? Or had I wanted to endow this meeting with an aura of ceremony so that, unlike last time, we might both feel more at ease?

I set down his sandwich and then a plate of the biscuits. He looks up. 'Ginger is my favourite,' he says.

'Mine, too.'

'Good for the digestion.'

'Are you worried about your digestion, Jurko? You've mentioned it before. Do you have a problem with it?'

'Not yet. But the fire in your gizzards is what keeps you alive. Not your heart, not your brain'—tapping the matted hair on the top of his head—'these are overrated. The furnace,' he says, patting his abdomen, 'the fire rises, yuh?'

I ignore this and point to a printout of the Knidos labyrinth. 'Look at this one, discovered just a few years ago in southern Turkey. Similar to the seed pattern but with one important difference. See.' I point to the centre of the design, not the geometric centre but the space where the path in arrives and the meander reverses itself, back to the opening. 'The Knidos has a circular space at the centre that's empty. You could put something interesting there.'

Jurko picks up the sheet and studies it for a moment, then lays it back on the table, shaking his head. 'Put nothing,' he says.

'Why?'

'Whatever you put there will own you.'

'How?'

'Look at these people with statues in their garden. That's who they are, these statues. Same with churches. Angels, Jesus on two bits of wood'—he holds his index fingers up in the shape of a cross—'gargoyles. All this nonsense.'

'Let's build it and we'll see.' I hand him a cluster of sheets stapled together. 'There's a website that shows you how to build the Knidos. It gives you detailed diagrams and instructions. Stone boundaries and the paths filled with gravel, or sand, or mulch. To prevent the growth of weeds.'

Jurko shakes his head, and points to another of the sheets on the table, a version of the seed pattern but not laid out with stones or pavement. Instead, it's made of earthworks built to form a low mound of around forty-five centimetres to sixty centimetres. 'This is maybe good, I think.'

'How would you do it?'

He shrugs. 'They have dug out the path, see, and then you pile up the dirt beside it. Then maybe you box the dirt, or maybe brick it in, or just leave as is, except maybe you get a big rain and the dirt wash away.' He reflects for a moment. 'You need concrete footings, I think. Then it last.'

'Concrete footings? But that would be...' I hesitate. The word *permanent* is on my tongue, and for the first time I consider whether anything lasting is what I want. 'It's quite a construction,' I say. And labour intensive, I think. I read the text below the image and it describes the low earthworks as a henge. And I like this word: the word itself, more than the design, speaks to me. Still I am sceptical. 'I don't think that would work,' I say, 'not behind the dunes. The sand is too volatile and the winds too strong.'

He shrugs again. 'Yes, so concrete footings you need.'

I rest my chin on the palm of my hand and am silent.

Jurko persists. 'Sand is the best foundation for concrete. Will not shift in the heat, or when wet. Clay is a problem. Up on the headland here is clay, yuh? But this clay shrinks in the dry and expands when it's wet.'

And I am struck by the paradox here: sand so volatile in its essence and yet so firm a basis for the rigidity of concrete.

'And there is another problem. With stone walls you trip over them in the dark. You break a leg.'

'I'd use a torch.' One of the websites I have consulted suggests a gas lantern at the centre to illuminate the labyrinth at night but I intuit that Jurko would not approve of this. And it would make me a target for the youths who come to the dunes at night to drink. They might very well vandalise the lantern, or use it for target practice. Most likely I would come out in the mornings and find empty tinnies pelted at it overnight. Already I have enough to clean up at weekends.

Jurko is still talking. 'Another thing. You could get some stones and maybe mortar them to the height of your ankle. You don't need concrete footing for this.'

'How would that work?'

'You build a shallow trench, not very deep, just a few mills.' He indicates the depth with finger and thumb. 'You can lay mortar straight onto the sand if you want. Then you gravel the path.'

I have a sudden thought. 'Curved walls,' I say. 'They must be more complicated to build than straight.'

He nods. 'Yuh, but no problem. This I have done many times.'

Now I am tired, and have begun to feel a peculiar resistance, as if the labyrinth was only ever meant to remain an idea, an image in a dream. But Jurko is pointing to the seed pattern. 'I tell you what I think. I think you start here, and you make it one day with stones. You live with it, a few weeks, maybe more, and you see how you feel. Maybe you don't like the design and you want something else. Or maybe you don't get the size right. You want it bigger, or you want it smaller. You get a feel for it.' He looks over to the sandy gap between the shack and the dunes. 'You should do this before you make something permanent.

Not to make a mistake.'

'Would you help me with this?'

'Of course. We stake it out with string and then place the stones. We do it in a day, maybe an afternoon.'

'This temporary labyrinth, Jurko. Where would we get the stones?'

'We collect from the beach.'

'What? Here?'

He shakes his head. 'We go to the beach behind Rittlers Point where nobody goes, only surfers. Lots of stones there the right size, and smooth. So many there, no one will notice the difference.'

'But that's illegal. Already that beach is eroding.'

'We don't worry. We borrow them. We return them later.'

'How many circuits?' We need to decide this in order to do a rough calculation of how many stones we will need. In theory the seed pattern is limitless, though online sites limit themselves to recommending three, seven, eleven or fifteen circuits. Jurko is quick to agree that three is not enough and would be merely decorative—'not serious'— and fifteen would be too many for a temporary labyrinth. We agree on nine.

'But that's a lot of stones.'

He shrugs. 'Up to you. You have a wagon so three, maybe four boot loads. They don't have to be big or heavy, and so many there, like I say no one will notice the difference. I stake out the yard with string and then we place the stones at intervals and you live with this awhile and see if you like.'

I hesitate. My mouth is dry.

'You could buy from the gravel yard at Marooka but that place is closed for four weeks, and good, I think, to strike while your iron is hot.'

'Okay, okay.' The word *henge* is echoing in my head. 'What if I did decide on a henge, Jurko? How would you do the stonework?'

'We talk about this another day. I have no tools with me. I have to borrow. We need to think more, but not yet.'

It occurs to me now that I haven't asked him about his price. How much does he charge for an hour?

'I stake out the simple one for nothing.'

'That's very good of you.'

'Is not a big job. After that, if you want stonework we can discuss. Depends on degree of difficulty.'

'So when would you like to start?' Before long he might not still be here. Sooner or later the park rangers will move him on. Understaffed as they are, one of them must eventually spot the tent.

'For three days I am cutting wood for Joe out the back of Mt Godwin. We could collect stones next Monday. I am free at the weekend but more surfers around then, so best to go on a working day.'

'Good. Monday it is.'

It's late afternoon. We have been absorbed for almost three hours. My shoulders sag; my back aches. Yet in a relatively short time so many decisions have been made. When I offer to drive Jurko home he says that he is stiff from sitting and would like to go for a swim. I think this is a good idea, not least because it will wash away the smear of mayonnaise and the piece of egg lodged in his beard. I fetch a towel from the linen cupboard and as he heads towards the dunes I call out, 'Watch out for the rip. Better to swim in the lagoon.' But he waves at me dismissively.

In no more than forty minutes he has returned to ask if he can have a shower, and I say yes, and get up to find him a second towel. Making no attempt to remove the wet sand from his feet he strolls down the hall to the bathroom in a way that gives me a momentary stab of annoyance. There he is again: too at ease. That boundaries problem.

When he emerges from the shower I am pleased to see that he has washed his hair. 'You can drop me at Medea Street if that is convenient,' he says. 'My bike is there and I am seeing Amy tonight for supper.'

So, he has a girlfriend. I find this reassuring. 'You like Amy?'

'She ask me to fix her downpipe.'

'Oh.'

'I take what work I can get.'

'Of course.'

When I lock the side door behind us, he says: 'Why do you lock? Who would steal from this place?'

'It's not theft I worry about, Jurko—it's vandalism. The local kids roam around the dunes at night because they're bored.'

'Of course they are bored. They have no work. They are not trained. They are shit.'

'They are *not* shit, Jurko. That's offensive.' I wonder if shit is what he means, if something here is lost in translation.

'You are what you can do. Otherwise'—he shrugs—'you are passenger on the bus.'

'Not everyone has opportunities, Jurko. You've been taught a skill.'

I wait for the inevitable comeback but instead he is silent. We climb into the wagon and as we pull out of the drive I see Ray Gittus on his veranda. This time he is not looking through me but is staring at the car, curious despite himself. I toot the horn and give an exaggeratedly cheerful wave.

By the time I return home, daylight has faded. The clouds that had deepened from coral to crimson are now a shadowy charcoal and the moon is a silver ball low on the horizon. The kitchen is warm and the light from its low-hanging pendant globe pools around the old pine table. Books and papers are scattered beside a brass bowl of scarlet and gold pin-cushion flowers that shimmer with reflected light, so that the scene is like a tableau of something fruitful in the gloom of a cave. From behind the dunes comes the sound of the sea, its soft rhythmic surge. At the window, a bogong moth is beating its wings against the glass.

I shower in my cramped shower bay, a cream-coloured recess that looks like an open capsule, rounded and shallow so that my elbows nudge the taps and my nose is only inches from the wall. A thin crack runs around the base of the capsule. Strands of Jurko's hair cling to its sides.

o

'Do you have any more drawings for me, Daniel?' In the past weeks there have been none, as if he has exhausted the life within his cell.

He does not look up but clears his throat, spits into his cupped hands and rubs them on his sleeves.

I glance across at the warder on the door. Today, for some reason, there is only one, an older man with dark circles under his eyes. When he had ushered Daniel into the room he had given me a look of melancholy sympathy.

'I'm building a labyrinth, Daniel.' The minute I say this I regret it. I know that on these occasions I should say nothing about myself. It's a provocation.

He doesn't look down but stares ahead at the crudely painted mountain in the mural behind me.

Too late, and I must go on with this. 'I was hoping maybe to interest you in it.' I take a folded sheet from my pocket and lay it out on the steel table. 'It's called the seed pattern.'

The warder inclines his head to look at the sheet.

'A few friends are going to help me,' I say. 'We're going to collect some stones from the beach and lay out a temporary pattern.' I point to the paper on the table. 'This one.' Then I

take a second sheet from my pocket, a photograph of the gap between my door and the dunes. 'Here.' Until now I've said nothing about the shack and to mention it now is to dig myself further into the pit of his silence. But my newfound enthusiasm has undermined my willed composure, and to make matters worse I am lying and my voice has a hollow, tinny sound, a ghastly false inflection I could almost choke on. I had once resolved that, no matter what, I would not lie to him.

'Your grandfather believed in making things,' I say.

There is a sadness in his eyes now. If only I had known him, he said to me once, when he was in his early twenties and I had taken some things out of storage, including my old doll's house. Daniel had come around one afternoon and found it sitting at one end of the dining table. He seemed delighted by it. It's so well made, he said, smiling, and peering into its genteel vestibule had exclaimed at the detail on the miniature staircase. He must have had some good tools, he said. And then: Where are they now? Your uncle sold them, I said. We had nowhere to store them. And Daniel had looked up and scowled. How could you let him do that? (Yes, how could I?) I would have killed for them, he said.

We have regressed. No more drawings. The drawings were a sign of life, and now they have stopped. Then it occurs to me, the obvious. 'Have you any pastels left, Daniel?'

He shakes his head. And I am relieved. There is hope in this, this normal human gesture. He has for a moment forgotten himself.

Time is up. I stand, and leave the printout of the seed

pattern behind on the table. Perhaps one of the warders will take it to his cell. Then he might relent and redraw the pattern in his own hand. I will send him a second box of oil pastels. I will restore his work to him, for there is no other hope than this.

o

Monday morning I collect Jurko at nine. This is the best time, he said, because the surfers will be there just after dawn, before work, but by nine they will be gone. Still, I am nervous that one of them might still appear over the steep dunes. I am sure that the gathering of stones must be illegal.

We drive to the long beach around the corner from Rittlers Point. Fringed with sandhills dense with boobialla, its long stretch of white sand is punctuated with crenellated layers of pockmarked rock that look like small terraced cities in miniature. The surf is roiling and the waves are churning up sand into a foam of yellowish scum. Further up the beach, great swathes of seaweed have been washed ashore but where the main track comes out there are patches covered in shells and smooth stones.

We squat by the tideline, where the shells and rocks are plentiful. Almost immediately a rogue wave washes in over my feet and up to my knees. 'Watch out for the seventh wave,' jokes Jurko. 'It sweep you out, maybe, and you drown, for sure.'

For an hour we collect stones and place them in

hessian bags and plastic buckets. I am ill at ease and collect in short bursts, throwing everything that looks vaguely suitable into my bucket and moving from one patch to the next until I am halfway up the beach and some distance from Jurko who, with what I have come to recognise as his usual intensity, fossicks for a long time in one patch, sorting carefully.

Already it is warm and humid but with a light south-easterly breeze blowing in off the water. In our absorption, I think, we are like children. When we have lugged the last bucketload of stones to the car I suggest we stop at an odd little coffee shop just off the highway. The café is also a musty second-hand bookshop, its shelves stuffed with crime thrillers and old history books that no one will ever read again. Jurko picks up a dog-eared and dusty book that lies on the windowsill, looks at it disdainfully and puts it back. I remember that he had been reading when first I approached his camp at the outlet of the Prince Henry River. What was that book? I had wanted to ask but not to pry, had caught a glimpse of the open page but it was not in English, or any language I recognised, so he must have brought the book with him, in which case it has special meaning for him and is probably still among his things.

It's just after 3 p.m. when we arrive home with the fourth load and together empty the boot and the back of the wagon, where I had thrown an old blanket over our contraband. We lay the stones out on the concrete terrace and Jurko washes the sand off them with the garden hose. When I look up I see Ray watching us from his veranda. This time I don't wave and instead go inside to prepare lunch for Jurko. The stones dry quickly and before long he is stacking them in a pile at the rear of the house. 'I start next Monday,' he says. 'The rest of the week I work at Powranna cutting wood.'

'In the bush?'

'Yuh.'

I know what that means. He is working for a wood-cutter who poaches timber from Crown land.

'Be careful.'

'Is all right. I am used to chainsaw.'

'I don't mean that.'

'Is okay. Joe pay the fine if we are caught, not me.'

It's not the fine I am thinking of. The police will check his visa, and if he has overstayed it. Or never had one.

○

Early evening, and I walk up the hill to Diana's house. Diana has rung to say that her daughter has arrived for the weekend and she wants me to meet her. A north-easterly front has moved in and a light rain mist is drifting down from the hills. Through her kitchen window, Diana sees me approach and comes out to wave me in.

Beside the big picture window of the living room a young woman is sitting on the couch.

'This is my darling Ingrid,' says Diana, and flaps her

hand in a most un-Diana-like way. She seems ill at ease. Ingrid is tall and blond and handsome and does not in any way resemble the dark, sharp looks of her mother. 'Ing's a lawyer, she's the one in the family with the brains, but you'd rather be an artist, wouldn't you, Ing?'

'Oh, for fuck's sake!' Ingrid turns away to stare out the window. Then, suddenly, she gets up, opens the door to the deck and goes out to stand in the far corner where she lights up a cigarette.

Her mother gazes at her through the glass. 'Just like her father. Nothing is ever good enough. I cleaned up the house for her. I even cooked.'

This is the first time I have heard a word spoken in anger about the late Max. *Nothing is ever good enough.* Meanwhile Diana has walked across to the kitchen and reached for a bottle by the sink. 'Brandy?'

I shake my head, and look over to the deck where Ingrid is staring out to sea. 'How long is she here for?'

'The weekend. She comes here when she's dropped her bundle. The rest of the time I hardly ever hear from her. Maybe once a fortnight, if I'm lucky.'

'It might be best if I go. We can catch up later.' I pause at the back door and wave. 'Best of luck.'

By the time I reach the bottom of the hill the mist has blanketed the paddocks ahead of me and a light rain has begun to fall. I open a cleanskin and carry it through into the sunroom to read through my latest notes, but almost immediately hear voices, a soft tread outside my window and then shouts from the dunes, and I know that in the morning my land will be littered with empty stubbies and squashed cans of mixer drinks. Shrieks and shouts of profanity will penetrate my sleep, and the occasional scream, and before bed I will double-check the locks on my doors and windows. But for now I am able to block it out by attending to my notes. *The constant reversal of direction, yet inevitably leading to the centre which becomes a place where all resistance can fall away…* There is an argument going on in the dunes, the sound of male voices shouting obscenities, and I get up to shut the window. *The maze is a form of torment, a prison, but the labyrinth is a mandala, the representation of a perfect state, the reconciliation and union of opposites where all contradictions are united: masculine and feminine, right and wrong.* A bottle smashes against my terrace. Then another. Right, that's enough. I get up out of my chair and fling open the side door that leads out to the concrete terrace. But now it is preternaturally quiet, with not even the sound of the sea. I wait, and wait. Silence prevails.

In the morning I lie in bed and listen to the sounds of the day: a car horn blaring, the wind howling, the rackety squawk of a wattlebird. The wind drops and a female wren comes to perch on the sill of my bedroom window and pecks at the glass, then scrambles up to the top of the window only to fall back down again, then the climb up again like some tiny demented mountaineer as if my bedroom window is the wren's Eiger, her Everest. Up, scramble, fall down, tiny claws raking against the glass, up again, down, over and over…

It's just after eight in the evening, the rain has eased, and I am preparing a late supper. I look out the window and observe a figure walking up the drive, a woman, an unfamiliar shape, and then I see that it's Ingrid Crosland. I open the back door and Ingrid stops, smiles diffidently and says: 'Oh, hi. I was just going for a stroll and thought I'd drop by. I hope I'm not interrupting anything.'

'No, come in.'

Ingrid doesn't move. 'I want to apologise for last night. At Mum's house. I was rude.'

'Yes, you were.' There is something in her eyes, a sad anger. 'Would you like a drink?'

Ingrid hesitates, then steps across the threshold and looks around her. 'This is nice.'

'Nice enough.'

'It has character.'

'Whatever that means.'

She grins. 'I think it means unrenovated.'

'Exactly. And will remain so. Meanwhile it's called rustic. Red or white?'

We settle at the kitchen table, where Ingrid makes short work of the first glass, suggesting that she is not so unlike her mother after all. Meanwhile I am waiting for her to establish the terms of this visit. Is she curious about me, or desperate to escape her mother's company? Her hand rests around the curve of her glass and I note the immaculate nails, painted a soft coral shade. She must, I think, frequent one of those salons where young Vietnamese or Filipino women in surgical masks attend to the hands of clients who sit back like queens on a rented throne, and stare at the evolving perfection emerging from their fingertips.

'Do you miss the city?' she asks.

'Not at all. But at my age everything is different. You would most likely be bored here. You have your career.'

'Oh, yes, my brilliant career.'

'Intellectual property, your mother tells me.'

'Yes. Fascinating. One company arguing with another over the use of a blue and white cow for their logo.'

'I imagine you work long hours.'

'I live my life in front of a computer screen and then I go to the gym.' She drains her second glass. 'Max—my father—wanted me to be a lawyer.'

'And you?'

Ingrid shrugs. 'I earn good money but I don't have time to spend it.'

'Save and you can retire early and please yourself.' I sound like a machine in an arcade, dispensing advice on a card. Something is bothering the girl, needling under her skin. We are speaking in code, the polite talk that wants to break through into somewhere else, that waits—hopes—for an opening. 'Do you have a boyfriend, Ingrid?'

We are on the third glass now and out it comes. Ingrid

is having an affair with her boss, Gavin, a partner in the big corporate firm she works for. She feels sorry for Gavin (of course she does). He is a decent, sensitive man, she says, but corroded by the contempt he feels for his clients, by their greed. For a while, she says, Gavin had sought counselling, and she explains the careful system established by lawyers among themselves so that they can visit a psychologist engaged by the Law Society, but in secrecy so that they can navigate the entrances and exits, the doorways and corridors of the building in such a way that they need never run into one another and be outed for their weakness. They are copper furnaces with holes punched through their skin and they are leaking. But Gavin's counselling didn't work, and meanwhile he has a wife and two children. Ingrid is his only solace (of course he would say that, and it's probably true; never mind that he hollows her out).

And how does Ingrid manage her own stress? She swims, she says, at the local pool, an hour in the morning, and as she talks, I can see her long, heavy body in the water, the steady stroke, arm over arm, the rhythmic breathing, the body pushing on, powering down her lane between the thin blue lines. A strong swimmer, like her mother.

'Have you been for a swim here?' I ask.

'Went for a body surf this morning.'

'You know there's a bad rip at the northern end?'

'So Mum said. Have you been caught?'

'I never swim in the ocean. Only in the lagoon.'

'Mum was caught in that rip once and it took her two hours to get back in. In the dark.' She smiles.

'Your mother has stamina.'

Ingrid bites her lip. 'Yeah, she's physically very strong.'

There's something about the emphasis she gives to *physically* that implies a judgement, a subtext that is better left unexcavated. I tap her on the arm, lightly. 'I would like to have had a daughter,' I say, and what I mean is: your mother loves you.

'So would I. I mean, I would like to have one in the future.'

Now, at last, we arrive there, in the space of true yearning. She is sad that no man in her world wants to have children with her. She is thirty-four and knows that time is running away from her, is haunted by the fear that her pursuit of it will prove futile. A woman in her prime, running up the beach against a gathering headwind.

'You know, it's possible to have a good life without children. They can be a source of great pain.'

Ingrid stares at me. She is not convinced; her body tells her otherwise.

'What does your mother think?'

'She thinks I should, in her words, go for it now.'

Yes, that sounds like Diana. 'You mean get yourself pregnant and have a child on your own?'

'Something like that.'

'And hire a nanny?'

'I couldn't afford one. Mum says she'd come and live

163

with me and help out.' She laughs. 'But I couldn't live with Diana.' She gives a look that says it all. 'You have no idea what Dad had to put up with.' She sighs. 'And anyway, it's not how I do things.'

I could ask what she means by this but I already know. Ingrid is thorough, methodical and above all responsible. She would like her child to have a father, and she would like that father to be a man she loves.

'What about you?' Ingrid asks. She is being polite. Don't talk about yourself for too long: take an interest in the other person. But this is an unnecessary feint.

'What about me?'

'Mum says you're building a labyrinth.'

'Planning to.'

'Like in Chartres Cathedral?'

'Not exactly. Have you been there?'

'Yes, on a school trip once.'

'And you saw the labyrinth?'

'No. After all the build-up and our teacher banging on about it we could hardly see it, never mind walk it. It was covered in chairs.'

'So I'm told.'

'It's very impressive. Kind of interesting that they made such a fuss of the Virgin Mary while keeping women in their place the rest of the time.'

I think of Jurko and smile. 'Sounds like the chairs are about keeping *everyone* in their place.'

Ingrid laughs. 'No walking on the grass.' Then, 'Mum

says you have a son.'

'I rarely see him.' And it's time to deflect the conversation from that subject. I sit back in my chair and sigh in a way that I hope will indicate the evening is over. But Ingrid is not in a mood to leave. 'I haven't told Mum this,' she says, 'but I'm thinking of having some of my eggs frozen.'

'I hear it's expensive.'

'It is. I went to an introductory session a while back and they served croissants. *Croissants!* Can you believe it!'

'I suppose they wanted to make it seem less clinical, to put you at ease.'

Ingrid shakes her head.

'Have you decided?'

'Not yet. It's not the money. I have the money.'

'But?'

'I guess I'm not ready.'

Not ready to freeze the flow of time. Caught in the drift of waiting for the father. 'Are we ever ready?'

'How do you mean? For children?'

'For anything.' Suddenly I am tired. *Ready for what?* All my life I have been ambushed, by both the good and the bad. Nothing has ever gone to plan. 'I sometimes wonder what "ready" means,' I say, and shake my head. 'Please come again before you leave. If you're in the mood.'

Ingrid takes the hint and rises.

'It's dark out there tonight,' I say. 'No moon. You won't see where you're going. I'll drive you home.'

'No, I'd really rather walk. But I will borrow a torch if you have one.'

I hand Ingrid my big torch that I keep in the laundry. I wave and watch from the doorway as she walks towards the headland, a shadowy outline in the wake of a horizontal column of light. She has a stately walk, with an elegant gravitas that if I were her mother I would find heartbreaking. I lock the door and return to the kitchen.

o

Hesitantly and with care I unfold a photograph of the labyrinth. 'It's just a trial,' I say. 'Stones from a beach near the shack.' I try to sound casual, to conceal my pride, but Daniel is not deceived and he gives me the look. The Daniel look, the look that puts out the light. He stares at me for a moment and then lifts his chin and laughs, and goes on laughing with a hard hysterical edge. Despite everything he is still able to mock me. And this is necessary, for who else is there to blame but mother? Then suddenly he lowers his chin, purses his lips and spits onto the glossy surface of the photo of the labyrinth. A phlegmy globule of saliva sits almost exactly at the point where the central cross of the pattern radiates out into its meandering pathways.

I could pick up the photo and crush it into a ball. I could ignore it and leave the defiled image lying on the table.

'It doesn't matter, Daniel,' I say. 'It makes no difference.'

'No, it doesn't matter,' he mimics. And again: 'It doesn't matter.' And these are the most words he has spoken to me in a long time.

I look up to the clock on the wall, the clock that makes no sound. I could smash that clock.

Out in the yard I am faint with nausea and have to lean against a wall. A guard walks towards me. 'You okay?' he asks. I nod, and head for the electronic gates.

At the rear of my car, with one hand on the chassis to steady me, in a sudden hot flush I vomit onto the gravel. I ate nothing this morning, so there is nothing to bring up other than a watery yellow bile. In the car I slump in the driver's seat and sit in a clammy sweat. All I can think of is the clock on the wall. Time is hollowed out, a maw that is swallowing me whole. I cannot escape it. There is no respite. I am deluded and I have been found out, hiding in a dream. The labyrinth is child's play. Like the doll's house. I will drive to the CO-OP in the morning and leave a message with Amy, for Jurko. And cash in an envelope, for his trouble.

Home, and I sit at the kitchen table and stare at the blank sheet of paper in front of me. *Time is a disease of the human psyche.* One of my father's precepts. Sane people live in the moment; they do not dwell on the past and they do not succumb to fantasies about the future. But on other occasions he would contradict himself. When people go mad, he would say, they step out of time because time has become unmanageable and everything is chaotic flux. They cannot put one foot in front of the other in any meaningful way. Nor can they make a decisive inter-vention in the sequence of time as measured in units by the society around them. Chronology defeats them. One disease generates another. The larger social disease—the yardstick and the clock, the endless computation—generates the smaller private one: a mad resistance.

I uncap my pen and I write Jurko a note. I assume he reads English and if he doesn't, Amy can read it for him. I find myself writing in a simple, almost child-like style I barely recognise as my own. 'Dear Jurko, I am too sad to go on with the labyrinth. I have had many worries and thought this might help but it hasn't. Thank you for your interest, your time and trouble. Erica.' I hesitate over that word 'worries': it sounds so banal, like an over-extended credit card or a dispute with a neighbour about a tree. But the note is a formality; it does not bear rewriting.

For the first time since I arrived in Garra Nalla I swallow a sleeping pill and go to bed early. And dream of a cathedral, of a long nave that extends all the way to the hills, a nave crammed with brown wooden chairs. Brown chairs everywhere, piled against pillars, and jammed up against a bare altar set behind a wooden screen. Mounds of chairs stacked so that they block the entrance, and the north and south transepts, a great ragged-edged tower of them, massed so precariously high that they block the light from the rose window at the end of the nave.

°

'Lexie?'

I am surprised to find the girl at my door. On the way

home from seeing Daniel I had stopped at Lexie's house and told her mother that I would not be needing her this week. 'Didn't you get my message?'

'Yes, but I left my hoodie here. I need it for a school excursion. We have to wear uniform.'

And I had meant to drop the hoodie in to her on my way to Daniel but had forgotten to put it in the car.

Lexie is carrying a white plastic shopping bag. 'Dad sent you these.'

Inside the bag is a jumble of figs, some purple, some half-green, some already bursting their skin to stick to the sides of the bag. They give off a sweet honeyed smell.

'Come in, Lexie.'

She looks at me blankly and then enters tentatively, as if unsure of her status.

'How were you planning to get home?'

'I've got a friend here. She said I could stay the night.'

'I see. Well, since you're here, would you like to do some work?'

'If you like. I'm up to M with the books. I was up to N but Jesse knocked over that big pile last time.'

'So he did.' The thought of Jesse makes me smile.

'Jesse's been sick.'

'He has?'

'He got pneumonia. He keeps taking his clothes off and he won't wear his shoes. We had to take him to the hospital at Brockwood. He couldn't breathe.'

'Is he all right now?'

'He's on antibiotics. Mum says he's accident-prone. He's broken both arms and he fractured a rib once when he slipped on the rocks and fell into the lagoon. He was lucky the tide didn't carry him out but that lady up on the hill was there in her kayak and she dived in and rescued him.'

'Diana Crosland?'

'Yeah, your friend.'

'I didn't know that.'

'Before you came. She was awful to him. Shouted at him on the beach and made him cry.'

'Well, better crying than dead. She probably wanted him to be more careful next time.'

Lexie is looking around her. 'I can stay till five,' she says.

For supper that night I eat the figs, too many of them. The sweet sticky syrup dribbles onto my chin and fingers, and I wash my face in the lukewarm water that trickles from the cold tap. Apart from the odd blustery shower the area has been in drought for eleven months.

Exhausted, I go to bed early again and for the first time in a long while sleep an unbroken sleep that lasts until dawn. When I wake my body is soft; it feels as if in my dreamless state I have known mercy, showered in unearned grace.

It must have been the figs.

°

All through the day I function in a kind of trance. What now? Well, nothing, and what does it matter? I have been here before, in the nothing time, and I will shelter in this old shack and sit passively under the weight of time, sit like a statue in a garden placed beneath the steady drip of water from a tap so that the moss grows slowly over its crown. And like a statue under the steady drip of hours I will accept that I have no control over anything.

It's just after six in the evening and I am beating eggs in a bowl when I hear a movement on the concrete terrace. I open the side door and Jurko is there. It's almost dark and he has cycled all the way from Powranna, where he has been cutting wood in the bush. The sweat runs from his forehead and drips into his beard, which is matted, shiny and damp.

'Jurko—'

He cuts me off abruptly. 'I bring this back,' he says, curtly, and hands me the envelope of cash I had left with Amy. 'Why you give up before you start?'

'Because my son is in prison.' There. I have blurted it out.

'Your *son* is in prison?' He is incredulous.

'Yes.'

'Why?'

'I'm not going to tell you.'

For once he is short of a word. Then he shrugs. 'I'm curious, of course. But is none of my business.'

I stare at a blowfly that is crawling up the flyscreen

on the open door. Just for the moment, I am that fly. *Go away, Jurko. This is all there is.*

Jurko's eyes are bloodshot. He looks exhausted.

'Your eyes,' I say.

'Some tree in the bush. I think maybe I am allergic.'

'Would you like some eye drops?'

'No, thank you. I have not come for eye drops. You should build this labyrinth, Erica. Being sad is not enough.'

'What did you say?' He has not called me by name before and the effect is startling.

He takes a cloth from his pocket and wipes his eyes. 'I said, being sad is not enough. Everyone is sad about something. You feel sorry for yourself. Fair enough, but everyone has a problem. And you don't have the problem of the castle.'

'What are you talking about, Jurko?'

'The castle. I tell you about it, then you change your mind.'

'I don't want to hear any of your stories, Jurko.'

'All right, up to you.'

'I'm making dinner. I'm hungry.'

'Okay, good.' He props his bike against the window and proceeds to take off his work boots. His socks have holes in the heels, and where his big toes protrude. 'You cook food, then we talk.'

Inside he sits at the kitchen table and rests his forehead in his hands. He seems uncomfortable, on edge. I, too, am uneasy, flustered by his sudden appearance. I will feed him and then say I am tired and ask him to leave. 'Please don't talk while I cook, Jurko,' I say, because at this moment I can't bear to hear another word from him. *My son won't speak to me and Jurko won't stop.*

I open a can of chickpeas and empty them into a pot, add spices with abandon because I can't be bothered to measure them out, chop spinach and boil rice and don't much care how it all turns out. In a small pan I fry a chicken thigh for myself.

'Ugh, the smell,' says Jurko. 'If you don't mind, I open the door.'

'If it offends you that much we can sit outside.'

We eat out on the terrace where mosquitoes buzz around the insect zapper I have somehow had the presence of mind to carry out from the pantry.

'Citronella is good,' says Jurko, disapprovingly.

'Only if you sit on top of it.' I am snappish. I wait for him to argue but he is hungry and wolfs down his dinner in silence. Then, as if dispensing with preliminaries, he turns to me with a look of intent.

'Now I tell you. The castle is the reason I leave my home.'

'The castle?'

'Yes, I leave my country because of the castle. Enough, I say—this is madness.'

'Jurko, what are you talking about?'

'The castle. I tell you about the castle. Then you see. You make the labyrinth.'

The night is quiet but for the zapper that goes *zzzt zzzt zzzt* as the mosquitoes career into its metal mesh. My head feels heavy and yet, now that we are settled, and I have eaten, I realise that I am pleased to see him. I take a deep breath. 'Where is this castle?'

'In a town you wouldn't know. It belong to a family of aristocrats who oppress the poor. Then the Nazis take it over, they make it into a prison. At the end of the war the partisans blow it up. But then some burghers decide they want to rebuild it.'

'Is this a heritage thing?'

'What heritage? They build just the façade and inside will be a hotel, and a shopping mall, all shops, everywhere. Probably Starbucks, even, yuh? But they have a problem. First they have to find enough stone masters to build this bad joke. My father and uncles want to sign on for the job and I say, no, not me. They say they work to restore honour but I say, you are all mad. So not me.'

'You could be working on this grand project and instead you're willing to work on a small private labyrinth in a nowhere place like this.'

'This is not a nowhere place. You really think that? Then why are you living here?'

'To be close to my son.'

He frowns, as if corrected. 'Ah, yes, of course.'

I smile, a smile of concession. 'Okay, I take your point about the castle but is that a reason to leave your home, Jurko? Don't you miss it? Your family?'

'I fight with my father and he beat me. He beat me bad. He break my face, my ribs.' He presses his hands, his long bony fingers, against his rib cage. 'I tell him I won't work for him any longer, not on the schloss. *I teach you everything. Everything!* he says.' He strikes the table with the flat of his hand and leaves it lying there, like a marker of something forever done with. '*Now you bugger me.*' He pauses. 'Sorry, bugger is wrong word. I can't translate.' He pauses, and then: 'He means I abuse his soul.'

I feel the breath catch in my chest. My son too has abused my soul. Worse, he has abused his own.

'This is why I come here, to Australia. I come to a country where there are no castles.'

I am light-headed, almost dizzy. We sit, in silence, and in those moments of silence that follow I begin at last to understand. He has been broken by his father, broken into exile. 'I'm sorry about your father, Jurko.'

'Yes, me too. So this is why you must make your labyrinth.'

'I don't see the connection.'

'I can't explain. My English is not enough. I don't have the words for this. You will see.' He sighs and rubs his bloodshot eyes. 'The castle is for big egos, but your labyrinth is for God.'

'I don't believe in God, Jurko, you know that.'

'You think that now, but you wait and see. Why do you build this thing? You could plant a garden. It cost you less and much prettier.'

'Not in this soil. Too dry, too sandy. Too much salty wind.' So hollow are these words that they sound in my ear like a muffled squib. And with a consciousness that I have not risen to the occasion, to what Jurko has offered, I lapse once again into the banality of the reasonable, so difficult is it to speak to the reality of my labyrinth dream.

Jurko persists. 'Doesn't matter. You could plant the natives—they survive here.' He shakes his head. 'You will see.'

'It's not what I want.'

'Exactly. So you will see.'

I could ask: see what? But this argument between us has hit a wall. 'How old are you, Jurko?'

'I am thirty-seven years in April.'

Too old to be humiliated without consequences. 'Have you ever been married?'

'No. And I would not want to have children of my own. Why bring children into *this* world? Too many already.'

'Perhaps. If they all survive.' I change the subject. 'My father had a castle of his own.'

'In which country?'

'Here. A hundred and twenty kilometres away. It was an asylum for the insane.'

'Your father was a madman?'

'No, a doctor.'

He stares at me, bemused. 'I don't understand this.'

'Never mind.' I stand, and take a deep breath.

'Jurko, would you like to stay the night?'

'Why do you ask this?'

'It's late. And I thought you might be tired of sleeping in a tent.'

'Tired of sleeping on the earth? Never. But thank you.'

And I am relieved. 'Then I'll drive you home.'

'Thank you. That would be good.' He hasn't mentioned the labyrinth again, and neither have I. Wordlessly, we have renewed our contract.

○

On the Saturday morning, early, we begin. We have agreed on a nine-circuit seed pattern because five is too small and eleven too large for a temporary form. The stones are mostly blue and grey, though some have a white marbled pattern and others a reddish tinge; some are smooth, others mottled and mostly they are ovoid like eggs, with rounded or flattened ends, though there is occasionally the perfect sphere or, less often, oblong. Some have a ridge down the middle like a white vein. Jurko piles them into the wheelbarrow I have borrowed from Lynnie and we wheel them to the centre of the gap. First we kneel and mark out the simple cross with four equal quadrants and then place a single stone in the outer corner of each quadrant. Jurko produces a tape from his leather kit bag and measures the distance between the cross and each cornerstone at fifty centimetres: 'Wide is good, plenty of room to walk and you have the room, so why not?'

Because I have decided on a left entry we first connect the top of the cross with the top right-hand corner stone. I think of us as 'we' but it is Jurko who squats on the sandy soil and places the stones that I hand to him from the mound in the barrow, pausing from time to time to swig at his water bottle. He moves to the top left-hand corner stone and begins to lay an arc of stones that joins up with the right horizontal line of the cross. The online directions said we would need to figure out how wide the paths would be and how much space the rocks would take up, and then find a stick with a branch that goes off at roughly a ninety-degree angle, and make one length at whatever width we wanted. *You might consider using a cubit, the length from your elbow to the tip of your extended middle finger for the width*, I had read. But Jurko had just said: 'We don't worry. We eyeball it.'

'You mean, *you* eyeball it?'

'Yes, I have the eye. Even my father admit this.'

And so we progress all morning and I see that it's true, that he does indeed have the eye and the emerging paths are of the same width, and what forms is a pleasing symmetry that I might have achieved alone but with a good deal more hesitancy and angst, a going backwards and forwards, a rearrangement of stones, a breaking of lines to reform the curves into their proper trajectory.

We pause for lunch which I bring out onto the terrace

and we say almost nothing, taking pleasure in the shape that has emerged, so simply and straightforwardly. Again I find myself contemplating an object that I might place at the centre, but silently because I know Jurko would argue and spoil the mood. ('The Old Testament was right about graven images,' he had said, when last the subject arose. 'Not many things but this, yes.') His is both a philosophical objection and an aesthetic one: anything at the centre must be tainted by a quality he can't name—'I don't have the English'—but I think he means to refer to some kind of kitsch, something impure; or a kind of altar, and hence evocative of the churches of which he so vehemently disapproves. When we had discussed the recently discovered Knidos design, found on the south-west coast of Turkey and carved into a small block of black marble, I had pointed to the inscription in Greek. KYRI BOETHEI: Lord help.

Jurko: 'See, it's Christian. Who is this Lord and what do you care?'

'I thought you believed in God.'

'God, yes, but God is not a Christian. And you say you don't believe, so this would be a lie.'

'Jurko, you are becoming a tyrant.'

'I just try to set you straight. But then'—he shrugged—'up to you.'

It is always 'up to you' but only after he has vehemently made his case.

In the late afternoon Diana comes down to look at the day's work.

'If the park rangers get wind of this you'll cop a big fine,' she says.

'We're going to return the stones.'

'When?'

'In a week. Maybe two. When we—I—have decided on what I want. The design. How big.'

'It looks good.'

'Want to walk it?'

'Sometime. Not now.'

'Drink?'

'Why not?' Diana looks around her. 'Where's Jurko?'

'He had a shower and then he rode off on his bike.'

'Last time I came he rode off as well. I don't think he likes me.'

'I don't think he does.'

When Diana has gone I linger outside to contemplate what seems now to be such a simple thing, and my brother comes to mind and our teasing play on the old labyrinth at Melton Park. And Ken interrupting our improvised play to set us tasks, and Axel complying, always the good child, and me standing off to one side, resistant to any limit set on my freedom.

Just after ten, I take the big torch out of the laundry cupboard and open the side door. I want my first walk in the labyrinth of stones to be in the dark. The moon is waxing gibbous and I scarcely need a torch. To my left is the soft charcoal outline of the hills, and at the bottom of the drive, across the road, the dark mass of a clump of blackwoods, the moonlight etching a tracery of their branches against the sky so that their shadows resemble a carved screen. I look down, and think of nothing, just the column of light on my feet, one foot after the other, and the grey sand and grey-green tufts of grass and weed that sprout between the silvery-grey stones, illuminated now by torchlight. But when I arrive at the centre it feels cramped, like a curved cage. This won't do. Perhaps if we enlarged the space at the centre I could place a wooden bench there and sit out in the warm moonlight. Yes. No more argument with Jurko. He will do as I say.

When I am back inside the house I look at the labyrinth again through the window, from a distance, and it's as though I am seeing it whole for the first time. And what I feel is a shock of recognition: it is as if my body has been laid on the ground in another form.

○

Just after lunch my phone rings. It's Jurko, ringing from a public phone booth in Brockwood. The park rangers have found his campsite and evicted him. And threatened him with a stiff fine if he is there when they return. 'They are kind, I think,' he says. 'They could have prosecuted me without a warning.'

'What will you do?'

'There is a camping ground at Brockwood, for tourists. I go there.'

I hesitate. *There are no beds in churches.* And I have a spare bed here. 'Okay,' is all I offer. At least he will have access to an ablutions block.

'I am cutting with Joe next week. Time for you to think what you do next.'

'I'm thinking.'

'Good. You let me know.'

The next morning my phone rings again. It's Jurko. He has had an argument with another man in the camping ground whose dog had barked all night. 'I tell him off. He want to fight me. The rules say no dogs but the manager blame me. I think he is a friend of the man with the dog. He tell me I am a troublemaker and to pack up.'

'Jurko, you know I have a spare bed.'

'No, no. Thank you. But I would camp for a while in your backyard, if that's okay.'

'Of course.'

'Thank you. I accept this offer. You are kind.'

'You can use my kitchen.'

'Thank you but you cook meat too often. No offence. I cook outside.'

'There are a lot of ants in my yard,' I warn him. 'In the sand. There are bull ants and jack jumpers and they have a terrible sting.'

'Is okay. I will deal with them.'

'All right, then. I'll collect you after lunch. Outside the CO-OP.'

It was only a matter of time.

On the beach I find Diana hauling her kayak out of the lagoon and tying it up to a nearby tea-tree. 'You're mad, Erica. You will regret this. You'll never get rid of him.'

'We'll see.'

When I get back from my walk I make myself a sandwich and then I drive south to the Brockwood caravan park, where Jurko will have packed up his camp and be waiting for me.

When we turn into my drive Lexie is there, squatting on the doorstep.

'Who is this?' asks Jurko in his peremptory fashion.

'A local girl who helps me with my housework.'

'This is a waste, I think. You don't have enough to do already.'

'Mind your manners, Jurko.'

'Well, I unpack.' And he climbs out of the car.

I relent. 'Come and meet Lexie.'

He offers the girl his hand to shake and she stares at it, then takes it for an awkward second before withdrawing her hand quickly, as if burnt, and sliding it into her sleeve.

'Choose a spot where you would like to pitch your tent,' I say. 'I'll make some tea.'

I banish Lexie to one of the spare rooms where there are still boxes of unpacked books and where she won't have to deal with Jurko.

Jurko decides on a spot behind the house and beside the big she-oak. 'Sheltered from the wind, I think,' he says, 'but not too close to the tree or the birds will shit on my tent.'

'Try it and see.' There are practical concerns we haven't even broached, like the fact that Lynnie and Ray Gittus will have a clear view of him, not that there is any by-law about camping on my property.

That night I insist that he eat with me. 'Are you cooking meat?' he asks.

'Not tonight.'

After dinner we sit on the terrace that now looks out over the labyrinth of stones. Jurko stands and stamps his boot on one of the long cracks in the concrete. 'This concrete is in bad shape,' he says. 'I could repair for you.'

'I hate concrete. I'd rather you broke it up and removed it, but not just now.'

'What's wrong with it? Not as good to look at as stone, for sure, but practical, I think.'

'It makes me think of bunkers, and parking lots.' *And prisons.* 'It's grey. It's lifeless.'

'You can paint.'

'The paint wears.'

'Depends how you use it. The Romans, they used it amazingly, yuh? The Colosseum, the aqueducts.'

'I thought they were made of stone.'

'No, no. The masons, they put a cladding on the concrete core. And look how it lasts. Steel will rust, yes? And wood rots, but concrete you can make strong.'

I fear I am about to get a lecture and change the subject. 'You haven't walked the labyrinth yet, Jurko.'

'No need. This is your thing. For me, is just a job.'

'I've been thinking about something more permanent.'

'Of course. This is the idea. This one temporary and then you decide for good.'

'I've been thinking, Jurko, about the henge.'

He frowns, and appears not to remember.

'You know. The low wall of stones we discussed, filled with earth and planted with herbs. I like the idea of stone walls. Not high, just around mid-calf.'

'What kind of stone?'

'I don't know. I thought you might have some ideas.'

'This you have to buy from a quarry.'

'Yes, of course.'

'You want cut stones?'

'No, I don't think so.' That would look suburban. Too neat, too finished.

'If you want herbs then you need what they call slipform.'

'Which is what?'

'You put up wooden planks either side and then you fill in with your rocks and mortar. But you will need concrete footings. And concrete, too, is poured between the rocks but you don't see because you put a layer of earth on top for your herbs. And you can point or not point.'

'Point?'

'You fill in the gaps between the stones with mortar so it look smooth. All together.'

'You can do this?'

'Of course, this is easy. But I tell you before, I need tools.'

'I can buy them for you. You give me a list and I'll go to the city and get them. I assume they won't be available in Brockwood.'

'Maybe. I try the hardware store and let you know.'

I reflect for a moment. 'I don't think I want pointing.'

'No, you want natural look. I think so too.'

Around nine I stack the dishes onto a tray, a gift from a friend many years ago. It's a roughly made rectangle of wood painted with a swirling pattern of two mermaids, each with an arm outstretched to the other in a configuration that evokes Jehovah bringing Adam to life on the ceiling of the Sistine Chapel.

'See,' I say to Jurko, 'like the Sistine Chapel.'

'I have been.' He grimaces. 'You get a pain in the neck from looking.'

He follows me indoors and while I stack the dishes beside the sink he wanders into the living room, where he begins what seems like an inspection of my furniture. He pauses by the mantel and stares at the photograph of Daniel as a boy.

'Your son, maybe?'

'Yes.'

He nods, as if comprehending something he couldn't possibly know. I wait for one of his direct questions but he frowns and says, 'I will go now.'

'Do you have everything you need?'

'Yes. Thank you.'

So now there is a strange man camped in my back-yard. From my bedroom window I can see the shadowy outline of his tent, lit from within by an LED light.

In the morning I walk outside to look for Jurko but his bicycle is gone.

After an early lunch I drive to Brockwood to do my weekly shopping and when I return Lexie is waiting on the doorstep, sitting hunched with her elbows on her knees and gazing out at Jesse, who is running in manic circles around the rockery.

Inside they lay their school backpacks on the kitchen table and I see a recorder protruding from Jesse's. 'What's this?' I ask. 'Do you play, Jesse?'

He nods.

'Would you play something for me?'

Jesse gives a self-assured nod, as if he is a veteran of the salon. He slides the cheap recorder out of his back-pack and takes up a straight-legged stance, feet together, beside the table. I wait, expecting something in the nature of 'Greensleeves', but instead an unfamiliar melody pipes out, something almost recognisably baroque in its clarity. It doesn't go for long and when he's done he holds the instrument loosely by his side. He is comfortable with it, like a boy comfortable with a tool or a weapon.

'That's lovely,' I say. 'Does it have a name?'

He hesitates, and casts a sidelong look at Lexie. Then says, with the innocent authority of rote learning: 'It's Bach.'

'Do you know who Bach is?'

'He's a German and he's dead.'

'Yes, dead for a long time.' It seems unfair that this boy should have all the personality in the family. I stifle an impulse to ask him if he knows where Germany is. I don't want to sound like an interrogator. Jesse meanwhile continues to stand to attention beside the table with a blank expectancy, as if he might be called on for an encore.

'Come into the pantry,' I say. 'I've bought you some chips.'

At that moment the flyscreen door opens and Jurko is there. 'Hello,' he says. 'Who is this?'

'This is Jesse, Lexie's brother.'

'Pleased to meet you, Jesse.' Jurko is uncharacteristically hearty and puts out his hand. Jesse hesitates and then shakes it. 'I am going to build something here, Jesse. You can come and help me if you like.'

Oh, really? Jurko is behaving as if he owns the place.

o

For the next week I barely see Jurko, for he is summoned by Joe the woodcutter. Quite how they communicate I don't know, as Jurko has no phone, but often he is absent on his bike and I assume they have a system for relaying messages, perhaps at the local post office, or through Amy at the CO-OP.

One night, after a visit to Diana for one of her rough dinners, I walk back down the hill by torchlight. As I approach my side door I half-expect the sound of my tread to bring Jurko out of his tent but nothing in the tent stirs. I have the distinct feeling he is not inside it. I look around for his bicycle and it's not there, despite it being late. Where could he be at this time of night?

Just after sunrise, I wake early and cannot resist checking to see if he is in his tent. I find him outside, making tea on his primus stove.

'Is everything okay, Jurko?'

'Sure, everything fine.' He squats on the grass, nursing his mug. He nods in the direction of the Gittus house. 'Who is that old guy over there?'

'Why do you ask?'

'He stares all the time. He stares at me. Anytime I look over he's staring at me.'

'Ignore him. He's sick. He's got nothing better to do.' I change the subject. 'I'm told there are two places around here where you can buy stone,' I say. 'I'd like to drive to them and have a look at what they've got. Would you have time to come with me?'

'Sure. We will do this whenever you like.'

In the morning we leave early to drive to a landscape business perched high on a windy hill that looks out to sea. There are cone-like mounds of sand and soils everywhere, like miniature Mt Fujis, and great walled compartments, open at one end, of sand and gravel. There are grey aggregate and blue-metal aggregate, which Jurko explains are for mixing in concrete, and red aggregate, which gives the concrete a reddish surface not unlike red granite. There are rose pebble, white pebble, gold pebble, onyx rock, white rock and endless samples set in wire cages. I am drawn to the Rustic River Pebble, to the roundness of the stones, their smooth edges and warm, subtle colours. But Jurko declares them to be too expensive. 'Also, too pretty—not right to have near your sandhills, your dune grass.' He gestures towards where a semicircle of plaster gnomes is arrayed beside the office door. 'Next you put one of these dwarf statues in the middle.'

'They're gnomes, Jurko, not dwarfs.'

'Same. Better I carve you a gargoyle than this.'

'You can carve in stone?'

'Yuh. Not good enough for cathedral but good enough for you.'

'Thanks.'

He waves dismissively at the pebbles. 'But this you don't want.'

I shiver, with a sudden intuition that I don't want anything here. The wind is chill and I am ready to leave. And I can see that he might be right about the river rocks. Their smooth round surface and the subtlety of their colouring is appealing in a loose pile but set into a wall would risk looking quaint.

Back in the car I ambush him. 'There is a labyrinth near here, Jurko. Would you mind if we stopped by and looked at it? I don't think it would take long.'

He shrugs. 'Sure. Might be interesting.'

Melanie Trask greets us in the middle of a small orchard of fruit and olive trees where she is pruning an apricot tree. She wears a long purple shift and her thick red hair is twisted up in a topknot wound with a purple ribbon. She is an imposing presence, tall and big-boned. As we approach she smiles, slips her secateurs into a hessian belt around her waist and gestures at the apricot. 'Did you know,' she says, 'that the Tree of Knowledge in the Garden of Eden was an apricot tree? There are no apple trees in the Middle East.'

'No, I didn't know that.'

'You must be Erica Marsden.'

'I am.'

Turning to Jurko: 'And you are?'

'This is my friend Jurko. He's a stonemason and he's going to build my labyrinth.'

'Oh, very good, very good. Lucky you. And have you

decided on a design, Erica?'

'Not yet. It's early days, which is why I'm grateful for the opportunity to look at yours. You can't really tell from books, or photos on the net.'

'Absolutely not. You must do the walking.' Melanie peels off her gloves and gives an imperious little nod. 'Come,' she says.

We follow her past a grove of flourishing olive trees and on to what looks like some kind of barn but is, she explains, a purpose-built enclosure for her labyrinth, which is spread out over the floor. The pattern of the labyrinth has been painted onto cloth and bought at great expense from a firm in Seattle.

'Canvas?'

'Yes. I can roll it up and transport it to just about anywhere for my workshops. Would you like to take your shoes off?'

She stands to one side while Jurko and I remove our sandals. Then she ushers us through the curtained doorway. Beyond the curtain she indicates a small wash-basin in an alcove, not unlike the fonts of holy water at the entrance to churches. 'Please wash your hands,' she says, speaking in low tones, and like a dutiful schoolgirl I oblige and dry my hands on a towel embroidered with a pink lotus. Jurko takes a step back towards the door. 'My hands already are clean,' he says, stiffly.

Melanie hesitates, her lips in a barely perceptible pout. Then she extends an arm towards the canvas. 'This is a healing labyrinth.' Her voice has dropped almost to a whisper. 'We treat it as a temple. Some people like to light a candle as they walk it, others like to ring a bell, or burn a smudge-stick of wild sage.' She gives an encouraging little smile. 'One lady brought ice cubes with her and she'd frozen some flower buds in the cubes as a symbol of what was frozen inside her that needed to be melted.'

I give a tight little smile of my own. 'I'd just like to walk it, if that's okay.'

'Of course. Just do it in your own way and your own time.' Melanie's voice has adopted a singsong tone. Her manner has grown more formal by the minute, as if she might at any moment go into a trance. 'Just imagine as you walk that you are climbing the tree of your life. You might like to ask the labyrinth a question, and don't be surprised if an answer comes to you when you least expect it.'

I nod, but Jurko is stiff, and seems uncomfortable. 'You go,' he says. 'I wait outside.' In an instant he is gone.

Melanie is unfazed. 'At the centre of the labyrinth you can sometimes meet your ghosts,' she says. 'Your friend is not ready for them.'

'I'm happier doing it alone,' I say, and mean only to be polite. There are no ghosts here for me; the enclosure is suffocatingly hot and the sooner this is over with, the better. Without further ceremony I step up to the entry point and begin self-consciously to tread the path. It takes only a matter of minutes, perhaps ten, since I am not inclined to linger. The canvas has a coarse feel and the black, tar-like paint of the pattern is too thick and too bold.

'Very nice,' I say when I return to the entrance where Melanie awaits me with a knowing smile as if to say: There now, don't you feel better?

'Do you have any questions?'

And I feel I should ask something, as a courtesy, but am overcome by claustrophobia, a desire to get out into the fresh air, aware too that Jurko is wandering loose in the garden. Beside the door is a donation box, a shoebox sprayed with gold paint, and I fold a twenty-dollar note into the narrow slit that has been cut into the lid.

Outside, Melanie hands me a pamphlet with information on the workshops she runs on sacred dances to perform in the labyrinth, 'alone or with others'. Hearing our voices, Jurko has appeared from the olive grove and walks now behind us. At the gate Melanie opens her arms, encased in the flowing sleeves of her purple caftan, and says: 'Something will happen now. It always does when you walk the labyrinth.' And then: 'You are very welcome to come back anytime, and next time you might like to bring with you your Ariadne's thread. I encourage people to make their own, like a long charm bracelet, and string it with objects that are meaningful to you. A love letter, a ring, a favourite flower, whatever feels right at the time.'

A nod seems the only possible response. I climb into my car, where Jurko is already in the passenger seat. I turn the key in the ignition and as the engine starts up I raise my hand in a stiff salute to Melanie, who is smiling at us, a smile behind which, it seems to me now, there is a sly force.

Out on the freeway Jurko sits bolt upright. 'That woman, she thinks she is a witch!'

'I think the word you're looking for is priestess.'

'Yuh, well, she is a nut house.'

'Case. She is a nut *case*.'

'Same.'

'She has a beautiful garden.' I feel the need to defend her. 'I couldn't produce anything half as good, even if I had her fertile soil.'

'Yuh, well, this canvas is cheating, I think. Like a cartoon.'

Sometimes he surprises me. He is right, but I am not in the mood for a lecture from Jurko and am relieved when he falls asleep, as he so often does in the car.

It's a long drive home through the Napier Valley. The prison complex looks ghostly in the dusk, its tall lights incandescent above steel mesh and barbed wire. Further on, in the grazing paddocks, a line of bonfires has been lit from dead and dried-out blue gums. Bulldozed into piles they flicker now in glowing mounds of flame. All night they will burn like ritual pyres until nothing is left but a thick carpet of ash.

The next day, Jurko comes home with a hessian bag hanging from the handlebars of his bike. From the bag he produces a grey rock which he sets down on the concrete terrace.

'Local rock. A lot of it in the paddocks up in the hills. I can work with it.'

'It's not very attractive,' I say.

'It can be, if you split it and layer it in mortar. I show you later, but not now.'

That evening, through the open window in my bedroom I can hear Jurko in his tent. He is talking to someone. A visitor? I didn't hear a car approach so perhaps it's a local, someone who has walked up the drive. I am curious but do not want to appear to pry. Still, it's my property and I am entitled to know who comes and goes.

It's not yet dark, though soon will be, and on the pretence of watering the young river wattles beside the fence that I have planted in the hope they will grow quickly and obscure Ray Gittus's view, I walk outside and uncoil the hose. The flap of Jurko's tent is open to let in the air and I can see him sitting cross-legged on his inflated mattress, gesturing while he talks. It's a small tent and if there were anyone else inside I would surely see them, even at a glance.

The shuffle of the hose against the grass alerts him and he looks up and calls out. 'Erica?'

I can see that he is holding something against his ear. *A mobile phone!* I bend to peer into the tent. 'Jurko. Have you bought a phone?'

He stiffens, as if caught in the act, and instinctively I step back. I hear him say: 'I ring you later.' Then he crawls through the opening of the tent and straightens up beside it, looking abashed. 'Yes, I have a phone, three days. Amy wanted a new one so she offered me this for a good price.'

I can't resist. 'I thought you disapproved of them.'

'Well, Joe always complaining that he find it hard to contact me at short notice.' He shrugs. 'What can I do?'

I am pretty sure it wasn't Joe the woodman he was talking to just minutes before, as there was a tenderness in his voice. Still, none of my business. He's been in the area almost nine months and he must by now know people. I wonder what he paid Amy for the phone but don't like to ask.

'So I can ring you now.'

'If you like. But no point,' he looks around him, 'while I am here.'

'Still, I'd like your number.'

'Sure. I message you.'

'Okay. Thanks. It's a smartphone, I see.'

'Of course. Amy always have to have the latest.'

Now I must go on with the charade of watering and hope he doesn't notice that the ground around us is already damp from my earlier efforts. I tug at the coiled hose, dragging it towards the fence while suppressing a smile. Jurko with a smartphone. No more holy fool.

○

Daniel's mood has changed. He seems...what? There is no word for it. Cheerful? Nothing so hollow. Nevertheless there is a faint hint of quiet glee to him. Yes, glee, as if he has suddenly gained access to a secret he didn't know existed.

'You seem well.' Well is the best I can manage.

'You think so, Mother?' Always the mockery, but today without bitterness.

'Yes, I do.'

Silence.

'Have you anything left of your pastels?'

'A few stubs.'

'Would you like some more?'

'Yes, I would.'

Yes, I would. Those words sound uncommonly strange in their forthrightness, their lack of rage, of irony.

'The same colours as before?'

'No. Get me the sepia. And the Payne's grey.' He pauses. 'And the cadmium dark green. Six of each.'

Should I ask what he plans to do with them? Better not.

'I'll order them as soon as I get home.'

He smiles. 'And how is your labyrinth going?'

It takes my breath away. I hesitate, for it seems some kind of trap. How much to tell him? A little at a time, at least until I know the reason for the improvement in his mood. 'I laid it out with stones, you'll remember.' Any description of my plan for a henge sounds extravagantly ambitious. 'I'm still thinking about what to do next.'

But his eyes have clouded over, as if some word or thought has sent him into a reverie far removed from me. How brief the lifting of that cloud, and for the rest of our time we sit in the old familiar silence. Still, some kind of shift has taken place, and once I am back out in the car park my skin begins to tingle with intimations of change.

That night I ring Jodie Jackson, my contact in the support group. In the past, Jodie has indicated that her husband, Miller, is privy to all kinds of prison knowledge.

'My son, Daniel.'

'Oh, yes. Daniel.'

'I visited him today and he seemed different.' A deep breath. 'Better.'

'Oh, that's good. Lovely.'

No, not lovely. 'I wondered, Jodie, if something in Daniel's circumstances in prison has changed. And if you would be able to find out for me.'

'I can ask Miller if you like. He's in a different section from Daniel but he might know.'

She is so obliging. She owes me nothing. From where does this casual kindness originate? We are a fraternity of the damned.

○

Diana rings. 'Do you realise there's a big easterly storm coming in?' From her vantage point high on the headland she can see black clouds massed above the horizon.

Yes, I have seen the forecast.

'Last time this happened your property was flooded. You might want to drive to Brockwood and get some sandbags.'

'Did the water enter the house?' I wonder at this, given that the shack is set up on concrete block foundations.

'I can't remember.'

I decide not to bother. Already the house is darkening and the marshes behind me are bathed in a weird half-light, a yellowish grey. I climb to the top of the sand dunes and look out at the great purple and black clouds that hover ominously over the ocean. Then I walk back to the house and wait for Jurko to return from cutting wood. I warn him about the storm. 'Your tent,' I say.

'Is waterproof,' he says. 'We see.'

'Why don't you pack it up and bring it inside? Just in case.' He looks at me sternly. He is tired, and there are twigs in his matted hair and sweat stains across his back. 'Okay.'

I make up a bed for him in the back room, a dreary, cramped little space. He looks around at the bare brown Masonite walls and says: 'Like being inside a matchbox, I think.'

'You will be dry.'

I am relieved when he goes to bed early.

For an hour I sit up in bed and try to read but am unable to settle. The eaves creak in the howling wind and the roof shudders. In the distance the south headland is lit up by flares of lightning followed by the explosive boom of thunder. Throughout the night the storm threatens from a distance but I hear only the roar of the sea. There is no rain.

In the morning I go to the window and see that the house is shrouded in a white-out of sea mist. Swathes of rain fog have settled low in the ravines and gullies that run down to Garra Nalla from the hills around Mt Godwin. Jurko is still asleep, worn out by long hours of woodcutting and hauling. I listen at his door and can hear his light snore.

I put on a raincoat and walk down the drive and around the corner to where the lagoon meets the sea. Great surges of foam are washing in from the breakers, swirling in cross-currents and rising in crests and peaks before sweeping all the way up the lagoon, across the mouth of the river and into the low-lying paddocks of the grazing property beside me that is not, as I am, shielded by the dunes. Mounds of foam sit like dirty snow among the boobialla while an erratic breeze troubles their surface, so that they heave and tremble. On the other side of the lagoon the sandhills have been eroded to a height of three metres and the popular picnic point is entirely washed away.

Now comes the rain as the storm makes landfall, sheeting rain that drenches me in minutes. I run back to the house where Jurko is up and brewing his chai. I accept his offer of a cup, potent with thick slices of ginger and black cardamom seeds, and the burn of it makes me cough.

'Too strong for you, I think.'

'Not if I put more milk in it.' We might have been doing this for months.

I stand at the window, mesmerised by the rain. Soon the tank and gutters are overflowing in gushing streams. To make matters worse the water is pouring down the steep hill of the headland to the rocky swales along the bottom road, where the drainage is not adequate. Within minutes water is running in rivulets on the gravel road and onto my land, gouging deep gashes in my sandy driveway and banking up at the foot of the sandhills until the whole flat area of my land—the gap—is a lake six inches deep. I look across to where the rockery is flooded and see a whip snake slithering in panic across the surface of the water, searching for higher ground.

By now the water has begun to seep in through the back door, where the sand is level with the foundations, and the mat is saturated. Jurko peers through the glass panel of the door. 'There is a drain out there, yuh?'

'Yes.'

'I think maybe blocked by sticks and leaves.' He opens the side door a fraction because here at the side the water is not yet up to floor level, and he takes the rake left standing by the door and wades out barefoot, prepared to tread on God knows what, and begins to prod at the submerged ground where he thinks the drain might be, waiting for the feel, and the sound, of metal against metal and the spokes of the drain. The rain is heavier now, he is drenched, and I bang on the window and wave at him to come back in. Defeated, he retreats and I wait for him at the door with a towel. Then we stuff all of my towels at the two doorways, along with remnants of old carpet left behind in one of the back rooms.

There is nothing to do but sit it out while the rain continues to beat down on the corrugated iron roof. The power has cut out and I have no gas and cannot light the wood stove because the pump that heats the water is out of action. Around four in the afternoon I light two candles and sit a torch upright on the table in a vase, and we eat some bread and cheese and fruit. Later I light a fire in the fireplace, wrap defrosted pasties in foil and heat them on the coals, turning them constantly to prevent them from burning. Then with the old-fashioned toasting fork I toast some bread that we eat with apricot jam. Jurko sets up his primus stove and we heat water and make tea.

In the damp, humid air we sit at the kitchen table, in candlelight, and drink our tea. After he has drained his mug Jurko gets up and says: 'I show you something.' He walks down the hallway and returns with a hessian bag that he lays on the table, and from the bag produces the grey rock he had shown me before, fleetingly. Now, with some care, he sets it down beside my plate. 'Now I show you. You have paper?'

I get up to fetch some paper from my printer and return to sit beside him while he sketches a style of wall I have never seen before. Thin slabs of rock, like rough tiles, are laid into mortar with only their ends visible. 'We buy the big flat ones and I split,' he begins. 'Then I lay them into the mortar so you see only the ends, like slices of bread. I have seen this in the wall of a Japanese temple.' He points to my laptop that sits now at one end of the kitchen table. 'When the power come back on I show you. It look natural, blend in with the dunes and the grass. No roundness. You get it right, it looks like something the wind threw up.'

'How high would this wall be?'

'If you don't want a concrete base, then low. A hundred millimetres high and just seventy-five millimetres wide. The width maybe of one flat stone. Then earth between, what you call your henge, just enough for a plant, maybe a hundred millimetres. Then of course a hundred milli-metres wall the other side. And your path is three hundred millimetres, maybe three-fifty.' He makes quick sketchy lines on the paper, as if it is all decided upon. 'So each circuit is around six hundred mills on each side and you have two sides, yuh? So, all up, with your nine circuits, then fifteen metres.' He lays down his pencil and smiles. 'And you have the room.'

Yes, I can see how it might work: rough and yet deli-cate, makeshift and yet permanent, poor and yet elegant. I look up at him and smile, and he too is smiling. We have got there; we have arrived at the form. Effortlessly, and through that unspoken connection that has sustained us thus far.

'Where would we get these rocks?'

'We don't worry. Lexie's father has a big pile of them in his backyard.'

Lexie's father? Now I turn to him, sharp and suspicious. 'You've met Lexie's father?' Has he been trailing Lexie? Is this where he goes at night? She's underage, for Christ's sake.

'Yes, Terry. He is a friend of Joe.'

'I see.'

'We make him an offer. Get them cheap. He will deliver in his ute.'

'Can you do a sample for me of this wall?'

'Sure. No problem.'

All night it rains. I wake often to hear the torrent beating on the roof, a tinny rattling sound. Around three in the morning, and again just after five, I get up to check on the doors. The towels and carpet are saturated but most of the floor is dry. The water must be draining somewhere.

A dim light appears at my bedroom window and I drift back into sleep, and dream that I am standing in the upper storey of a plain suburban house and looking out the window, surrounded on all sides by deep water. The water is calm, with not a ripple on its surface that reaches to the horizon on all sides. The sun shines on the silver surface of this water, a sheet of stillness that reflects light back to the sun. A tall, slim man is standing in the room with his back to me. He is dressed in a dark suit, and he too is gazing out at the water. Water everywhere, and I am entirely without anxiety. But who is this man with his back to me? It's not Jurko, so who is it? And why is he there, since he does nothing but gaze at the water, at the stillness and the light?

I wake at seven to find that the rain has begun to ease, is still insistent but not as heavy. I turn on my battery-operated radio for the local news to learn that the inter-section where the highway turns off into Garra Nalla has been flooded to a depth of one and a half metres and the town is cut off, though the water is rapidly draining into the narrow river that runs into the lagoon.

By ten, the water around the house has subsided and I go out with Jurko to survey the sodden ground, Jurko in bare feet, I in an old pair of boots. Water from the head-land has flowed down the hill in a rush of gravel and mud. The turbid waters of the river on the grazing land have overflowed and littered the gap with debris, clumps of grass and branches torn from trees. The stones of the temporary labyrinth have been washed out of alignment and are scattered in the mud, barely discernible among the mire.

All morning we work at clearing the ground, removing the largest of the branches first and then collecting the stones from the dispersed labyrinth, fossicking among the bush litter with gloved hands, wary of what we might find. We stack the retrieved stones in a muddy pile beside the house until it seems that we have recovered all but a few. 'We wash them,' says Jurko, 'and when the ground dry out we start again.'

The smoky grey rain cloud is low, so low it looks like a woolly ceiling. Birds are beginning to reappear from wherever they sheltered and when Jurko and I walk down to the lagoon to survey the damage we find cormorants on the rocks, and a cluster of opportunistic pelicans on a sandbank, alert to the possibility of mullet swept in by a still roiling sea. Jobe, the young agent, is there with some mates, and he nods at me and beams. 'Awesome,' he says. 'Never seen it like this.'

Jurko and I return to the shack and resume the work of clearing debris. Jurko gets a call from Joe for help and I drive him to the turn-off to see if the road is still flooded, only to find that the waters have subsided, leaving in their wake a destroyed potato crop. Plants have been torn from the ground and swept onto the road, or hang bedraggled on the barbed-wire fences like bizarre tuberous fruit waiting to be plucked. I offer to drive Jurko to Joe but he says no, Joe can wait. 'First we finish, we clean up your yard.'

We return to the muck, and the swamp that is my home, and suddenly I am bone-tired and wishing that Jurko had gone off to help Joe. My arms ache, and my lower back. My feet drag and I stumble and trip on the torn-off branch of a she-oak, and falling forward I look up and out to steady myself, out over the paddock of drowned ferns between me and the Gittus property. And see Ray Gittus walking towards me in yellow gumboots.

For a moment I think I must be imagining it. Ray who never leaves the house other than to visit his doctor? Who never waves back? Who suffers from a mysterious withering of the will and who chooses this moment, of all possible moments, the muck and chaos of the flood, to make a neighbourly call. But perhaps Lynnie is in some kind of difficulty and he has finally had to rouse himself to get help. Or has he come to reprimand us for taking stones off the beach? The former fire warden has found some moral high ground and it has energised him.

'Ray. This is a surprise.' My tone is cool and I am nervous on Jurko's behalf.

'Bit wet for it.'

Is this an attempt at humour? 'Yes, well, as you can see, we're trying to clean up.'

Ray looks to Jurko. 'How's it going?'

I relent. 'This is my friend, Jurko.'

Jurko wipes a muddy hand on his shorts and offers it to Ray, who shakes it and gives another curt nod. 'G'day.' He stands with feet apart and arms folded, and says: 'Did yers hear about the potato crop?' He jerks his head in the direction of the drowned paddocks.

'Yes, we saw it.'

'The dam broke. That's why the road flooded. I told 'em that dam was in the wrong place when they built it. Washed away the entire crop. Spuds everywhere. Hangin' on the wire fences, filled up the culvert, spilled all across the road. Never seen anything like it.'

Jurko frowns. 'Bad luck, yuh?'

'Not bad luck, mate, bloody stupidity. I told 'em that dam was in the wrong place,' he says again. 'You should see it down there. The freeloaders have come from all directions. Shovellin' spuds into buckets, into the boots of their cars.'

'Good eating?' asks Jurko, as if this were a normal conversation about local produce.

'Don't ask me. The squatter's a miserable bastard. I wouldn't eat his spuds if I was starvin'.'

I smile despite myself. If anyone's a miserable bastard it's Ray. But is this why Ray has decided at last to acknowledge me, Ray who stares through me on my walks? Because he has a good story to tell, too good to resist, and a good story needs to be shared? Because someone else's misfortune has enlivened him? And does Lynnie know he's here?

'Well, we'd better get on with it,' I say. But Ray makes no attempt to leave.

'Saw yers workin' the other day. Markin' somethin' out.'

I explain briefly about the labyrinth. Now that I have recovered from the shock of his appearance I resent his intrusion and hope he will be put off by the esoteric nature of my project and retreat to his wicker throne on the veranda. Instead, he seems bent on conversation, though he turns down the corners of his mouth in a way that suggests he has no interest whatsoever in fancy garden plans. 'Where yer from?' he asks Jurko.

'I am from what you call the Balkans.'

'Oh, yeah. My old man fought in those parts in the war.'

'Excuse me but I think you make a mistake. The Allies were never there.'

'British navy. Off the coast.'

'Jurko's a stonemason,' I say. 'He's going to build the labyrinth for me.'

'Oh yeah. What with?'

'We haven't decided. We marked out a pattern the other day with rocks but the rain's washed them away.'

'Reckon you need a concrete base.' Ray kicks at a tuft of soggy grass protruding from the wet sand. 'This sand's an ideal base for concrete.'

Jurko looks at me.

'We haven't decided,' I say again.

'Reckon you do. Got a mixer in the garage you could borrow.'

'Thanks, Ray, I'll keep that in mind.'

'Mix it for yers if you like.'

I am speechless. I cannot get my mouth open.

Jurko shakes his head. 'I have mixed concrete many times myself.' He looks across to me. 'And she doesn't like concrete...' he begins, but I cut him off.

'That's very good of you, Ray, but we haven't decided on a design yet. It could take a while.' *What on earth is he doing here?* I look around, hoping Lynnie will appear and take him home. 'We won't be building it for some time now. Too much cleaning up to do.' And still I wait for Ray to leave, but Ray just stands there.

'I think I make some tea,' says Jurko.

Ray nods, as if this is some kind of invitation, as if by now he has sent down roots into my boggy sand and is a fixture of the place. Exasperated, I hear myself say: 'Would you like a cup, Ray?'

'If yer makin' one.'

I open the side door and Ray follows me in. He has removed his gumboots and enters in his bare feet, pale and pink. He looks around him. 'I knew the old bastard who owned this place,' he says. 'Wouldn't give you the time of day. But you have to feel a bit sorry for the man. His wife drowned off the beach. After that none of the family wanted to come here.'

'There's a bad rip here.'

'There sure is.'

Jurko has been listening to all this with a half-smile and wide eyes. 'I thought Australians never drown. All strong swimmers.'

Ray looks at me and nods in Jurko's direction. 'He's takin' the piss.' Then he looks back over his shoulder at Jurko. 'Yeah, well, they like to think they are, mate. They like to think a lot of things.' He turns back to me. 'Got any sugar?'

I take a jar from out of the cupboard and he heaps four teaspoons into his mug. Jurko winces. He doesn't approve of sugar. When Ray goes he will slap the table with his palm and say: 'You see that? Four teaspoons. No wonder that man is sick.'

Later, I will be unable to recall what we talked about.

All I had wanted was to find a polite way to get Ray out of my house but the encounter began to take on the quality of farce. Jurko had been talkative, as if it were he who was the man of the house and offering hospitality. He had wanted to know when the last flood was and why they had built the strange swales in the town made of sharp-edged stones, and question had followed question with Ray clearly enjoying his status as an authority until I had feigned a headache and said they would have to excuse me but I must lie down, and Ray had taken the hint. Soon after, Jurko had left to ride somewhere on his bike, parked now in my laundry.

He had not returned until late.

The next morning Lynnie is at my door. 'Please, Erica. Please, love. He hasn't been off that bloody veranda in months.' Her voice falters and she brushes at her wet eyes with irritation. 'If you could just find something for him to do. Anything.'

Luckily, Jurko has gone off to cut wood for Joe. 'I don't know, Lynnie. It's really up to Jurko.'

'I understand that, love. I do. I'll just leave it with you.'

'Ray offered to help with concreting, Lynnie, but I don't want concrete.'

'Yes, well, he gets an idea in his head and you can't budge it.' She pauses. 'He has done a bit of bricklaying in the past. Perhaps Jurko could show him how to set the stones.'

'Jurko's a bit of a control freak, Lynnie. I can't imagine him letting anyone do anything.'

Lynnie frowns. 'I'll think of something,' she says. 'Don't tell Ray I called.' She turns and begins to walk away, then stops, and looking back over her shoulder says, 'I don't know what it is but Ray's been more cheerful since the rain, more like his old self.'

○

After the storm the hot sun appears and the earth begins to dry. I drive to Brockwood for supplies and observe the remains of the potato crop, the plants caught on the jags of barbed-wire fencing, still hanging but already wilting. The dam wall is breached, cracked and clogged with mud. The million-dollar pivot sits stranded in the waterlogged field like a giant praying mantis with steel wings. The bright sun is mocking.

On my drive home from Brockwood, I get a call from Jodie Jackson. I pull over into the nearest layby and ring back.

'Any news, Jodie?'

'I saw Miller today.'

'Oh, good.'

'He says Daniel's made a friend.'

'A friend?'

'Yeah, a mate.' *Mate*. The word is imbued with a hideous irony.

'Did Miller say anything about who this friend was?'

'Yeah. You'd know him. Remember that doctor who strangled his wife? Roger someone.'

'Roger Kemp?'

'Yeah, him.'

'Good God! I knew him, once.'

'Yeah? Amazing, eh, how things turn out.'

As a young doctor from a prominent family, Roger Kemp had been a flamboyant man about town with a liking for rough trade and had rented rooms for his assignations at the Marshall hotel. In late middle age, he had married for the third time, a small, finely built Thai woman, much younger, whom he was said to dote on. 'For the first time in my life,' he had said at his trial, 'I was happy.' But he was a big man, and immensely strong, and in the sexual act had pursued the practice of pressing on his new wife's carotid artery in order to heighten her pleasure. On what the prosecution described as the fatal night he had pressed too hard. And rung the police, sobbing. 'Yes, I killed her,' he said repeatedly in his statements. 'Put me away.' And they did. The jury convicted him as much for his careless intemperance as for any belief in his malice. Manslaughter.

In Jodie's account, Roger Kemp is a popular figure in the prison, genial and always available for informal medical consultations. But the striking detail is this: he runs the prison library, and noting the calibre of the books borrowed by Daniel began to take an interest in him.

Daniel has been borrowing books? Daniel is still

reading? Hadn't he instructed me to burn his books? Now it seems he has permission to work in the prison library where mostly he sits and draws portraits of Roger Kemp, whom he sketches from every conceivable angle, portraits that he sticks on the walls of his cell. He has even traded some of these for, in Jodie's words, 'stuff'. What stuff? Who would want a portrait of Roger Kemp?

And how had Daniel got permission to do this? I can think of only one possible way, that Kemp has status in the prison. Of course. An educated and charismatic figure. A useful prisoner, a prisoner of influence who can protect his gifted acolyte.

'Sounds like your Daniel is a bit obsessed,' says Jodie. 'Is he gay?' she asks, as an afterthought.

'No. No, he's not gay. But thanks, Jodie, thanks so much. This helps.'

I do a quick calculation of Kemp's age and it comes to me. At last, Daniel has found a father figure.

o

Jurko returns from woodcutting. He brings with him a heavy tarpaulin, borrowed from Joe, to spread on the wet ground. Once again he sets up camp at the rear of the house. Inside returns to outside, and he seems determined to make a point, though I am baffled as to what it might be.

'Really, Jurko, there is no need,' I say, 'you are welcome to sleep inside.'

'I know this.'

On the Friday morning I find he has risen early. Out on the bare stretch of ground behind the dunes he has built a sample wall, one metre long. In an old tin bucket he has mixed a little mortar and cemented some split rocks into layers, each layer separated by two centimetres of mortar. And immediately I am smitten. Yes, it does look like something the wind blew together, and my concern that the mortar would look grey and ugly has proved to be unfounded: it's a warm earthy shade.

'The mortar,' I exclaim. 'It's a good colour.'

'I mix it with some yellow clay from behind Joe's house. It look good, yuh? You don't like concrete, you don't get concrete.'

I could weep. He really does know what he's doing. And I see that all along I have doubted him. He could so easily have been a fake, and the album of work that he showed me stolen from someone else.

A trio of black cockatoos screeches across the block between us and the Gittus house and I look up. Ray is out of his chair, standing on the veranda and staring across at us. He waves.

o

On Sunday morning, Lexie's father Terry arrives with the first load of rocks and for the next two days Jurko works at splitting them with a short blunt hammer and a long chisel, borrowed from Joe, until a neat pile of thin slices of rock is stacked against my rear wall. The sound of chisel against rock is the happiest sound I have heard since I came here.

Further along the wall are the stones from the beach which we have yet to return. Unwilling to distract Jurko from his work at splitting the rocks, I load some of the stones into my car and return them to the beach alone.

On the Tuesday, when Lexie arrives after school, we carry the remaining stones to the wagon and cart them back to the beach. After the third load I drop Lexie off beside the wooden angel at her gate.

°

The work begins.

On the first morning Ray brings his alarm clock with him to the construction site and sets it down on my weathered garden table.

Jurko frowns, and turns to me. 'What is this clock?'

'I don't know,' I say. 'Just ignore it.'

'No, I ask him. Is my worksite. I should know. What is this clock, Ray?'

Ray winks at him. 'Tells the time, mate.'

'You don't have a watch?'

'Don't like 'em.'

Jurko lets it lie. It's unlike him, I think, to display any tact, and I wonder if he feels some deference towards an older man. Something in his upbringing? Or perhaps he has heard about Ray in the district and feels sorry for him.

Later, I think, I will explain to Jurko what Lynnie once told me, that Ray sets the alarm to ring the hour. And if he's especially anxious, the quarter-hour. But on reflection I decide to say nothing. Let them sort it out.

But now they must mark out the pattern and this time with precision. First they drive in the five fixed vertical posts, wooden stakes cut in the bush by Joe. This time there is to be no trusting the eye; Ray holds the tall stake that Jurko has planted in the sand at the centre of the design while Jurko works outward with a ball of twine, marking the paths out with a series of smaller stakes since the ground is too sandy to retain chalk marks. This takes less than an hour, and before long Ray is mixing the mortar and Jurko is setting out a single layer of the thin, flat stones in the nine circuit curves marked out with the stakes. Tomorrow they will begin the work of laying the stone walls of the henge. And fill in the dirt when the nine circuits are done.

'Three weeks,' says Jurko, 'with Ray's help.'

And yes, I have to admit, though with ill will, that Ray is a godsend.

'What about Joe?' I ask.

'I tell him I have other work.' He grins. 'I tell him it pay better.'

In the evening I walk up to the headland for one of Diana's quirky dinners. Tonight it's anchovy toast followed by lemon slice, the one too salty and the other too sweet.

Diana is fretful. She has just had a call from Ingrid, who is infatuated with her new man. 'Off her tree,' says Diana.

'A lawyer?'

'No, a *baker*. Spends his nights kneading dough, apparently.'

'What kind of dough?'

'Honestly, Erica, only you would ask that question. Bread is bread.'

Bread is never just bread, and I am thinking that the daughter of a woman who doesn't care to cook might well be attracted to a man who does. 'How did they meet?'

'Tinder. He works at night so doesn't get to meet anyone much.' She sighs. 'I suppose he's an improvement on her first Tinder date. Some dud who disappeared to the lav to snort cocaine.'

We move to the table on Diana's deck that looks out over the blowhole. The giant boulders that frame its narrow gorge deepen in shadow while we nurse our gins, or at least I do: I have to walk home down a steep road where the gravel can sometimes give way underfoot.

'How's Jurko?'

'Good.'

'I saw him on his bike the other night, riding through Brockwood. It was after ten. Has he got a girlfriend?'

'I've no idea. I think sometimes he just goes for a ride.'

I don't pry into what Jurko does in his spare time. There are many things I could ask him but we seem to have arrived at an understanding, an intimate relationship peculiar to the labyrinth: we talk only about form, about tools and materials, and the effect of the weather. It occurred to me some time ago that Jurko never alludes to his mother, and I thought about how I might somehow bring her into the conversation, but decided against it. The past is the past. We have established our protocols and I would be a fool to disrupt them.

o

One morning, on my way to the beach, I turn a corner and there is Lewis Eames, returning with his dog from his own walk. It's an awkward moment. He said he would ring me when he returned from the city and he hasn't.

'How are you getting on with that labyrinth of yours?'

'I've found a young man to build it for me. A stonemason.'

'Oh? A local?'

'I don't think you'd know him.'

'I know most of them.'

'Trust me, Lewis, you wouldn't know this one.' I raise my hand in a polite wave. 'I'd better keep walking. The wind will come up soon.'

But in the late afternoon, around four-thirty, Lewis comes by to observe the works. He has some cheek, I think, but resolve not to show any rancour. Clearly he is curious, and though he has offered no gesture of friendship in the past, he strolls up the drive as if a familiar and says: 'This looks interesting.' He nods at Ray, who is feeding the cement mixer with sand and gravel. 'Ray.'

Ray neither looks up nor pauses. 'Lewis.'

Lewis turns to me. 'Your labyrinth, if I'm not mistaken.'

So pompous. 'Yes.'

'Coming along, I see.'

'Yes.'

'A bit of an unusual design.'

'It's a henge. And when it's finished I'll plant it with herbs.'

'Very dry here for most herbs.'

At this, Jurko looks up from his trowel work and surveys Lewis with a hostile stare.

'I'll seek advice,' I say hastily. For some reason Jurko and Ray are freezing Lewis out. Why? Where is the common currency of small-town civility? And I should forgive Lewis his lack of interest, indeed be grateful for it, for had he embarked on the project there might have been no Jurko. The thought prompts me to offer Lewis coffee. He accepts. 'Come into the kitchen,' I say.

While the mugs are warming I walk to the door and invite Ray and Jurko to take a break. 'Too busy for that,' says Ray, 'but thanks, love, you can just leave it outside on the table for us if you wouldn't mind.'

Love? Ray has never before called me 'love'; he is acting a part, assuming familiarity, and I can only assume it's for the visitor's benefit. I look across to Jurko who, tamping at the mortar, doesn't look up but is wearing a sly grin.

Why has Jurko allowed Ray in on his project? Why does he allow Ray to speak for him, even if it's only about coffee? I feel a pang of annoyance. Who is Ray to take on this tone? I should not have agreed to his participation but had been disarmed by Jurko. 'The old guy is harmless,' he had said. 'Give him something to do.' There is a subtext here, one between men, and I am being excluded from it.

I ask Lewis about his work on the surf club in Wynton. 'Steel and plate glass, I suppose.'

'And some stonework, if I can persuade them.'

Stonework? Ah, now I am interested. Perhaps I can persuade Lewis to employ Jurko. And it comes to me that when Jurko has completed the labyrinth I would like him to stick around.

When after forty minutes of polite conversation Lewis rises and I am able to wave him off at the door, I cannot avoid hearing Ray mutter under his breath: 'Bloody know-all.'

That evening, when Ray has gone home and Jurko is rinsing his tools at the garden tap, I say: 'You seem to be getting on well with Ray.'

'He remind me of one of my uncles, the only one I like. Uncle Pedja. He treat me fair. Not kind, but fair. Not his slave.'

'And Ray looks like him?'

Jurko shakes his head. 'No, no, not looks. Not that.'

On the first Saturday, Terry arrives in his ute with another load of stones, Lexie and Jesse beside him in the front seat.

I go out to greet them. 'Please stay,' I say to Lexie, 'if you're not doing anything. I can run you home. Jesse, too.'

But already Jesse has leapt out of the ute and is running across to where Jurko is laying a curve in the low wall.

Jurko looks up. 'You,' he says peremptorily, 'you can carry stones. Over there.' He points to the neatly stacked rows along the back wall of the house. 'You bring them to me.' Lexie he ignores.

'Come inside,' I say to the girl. 'You can help me make some sandwiches.'

'Lucky with the weather,' says Ray, to no one in particular.

On his way to the pile of cut stones Jesse pauses beside the outdoor table. Standing on his toes he reaches across to the centre of the table to pick up Ray's alarm clock, which sits in its usual spot. Ray, in the act of shovelling sand into the churning cement mixer, freezes his shovel in mid-air. 'Don't touch that, mate!' he barks.

The boy freezes. Lexie, at the door of the kitchen, stops, turns and walks over to Jesse, and putting an arm around his shoulders she ushers him away from the table and towards the pile of cut stones. There she bends to whisper something in his ear while Jesse stands transfixed. Clearly he is afraid of his uncle. When Lexie has finished whispering, Jesse nods, and she points to the stones. She waits, and watches as the boy stands on his toes to reach for the top layer, and her eyes follow him as, with great deliberation, a seriousness almost comical, he carries a stack of three across to Jurko. It's as if her gaze might cast a protective halo around him, such is her focus. Then, when she is satisfied that the boy is settled, is happy, she turns back towards the kitchen.

I say nothing, but there is a tightness in my chest and I am on the edge of tears, ambushed by an image, the sudden recollection of my arms around Axel, a feeling submerged in my unconscious that surfaces now like a storm creature rearing up through an ice floe. There was a time when I too had sought to console my younger brother. A brother I haven't seen or spoken to in a year.

Lexie is at my elbow. I point to the food laid out on the kitchen bench. 'Cheese and lettuce for Jurko,' I say. 'Ham for the rest of us.'

○

The weather is warm again and the persistent heat has dried the earth though the dams remain full. The days seem to pass in a haze, a rhythm of work in which the two men barely speak, either to one another or to me, and this absence of words is profoundly natural. And I stare in amazement at the uncoiling form of the labyrinth that seems almost to have a life now of its own, even as I hover on its fringes with sandwiches and coffee like an ageing handmaiden. Ray goes home for lunch and reappears at two in the afternoon and they work until, sometime around four, Jurko says: 'Enough, I think, for today.' Then Jurko washes his tools, has a shower and goes off on his bike for a long ride to God knows where. 'I stay fit,' is all he says. Sometimes he doesn't return until after ten and almost always he goes straight to his tent.

And in this interval of charmed days, time seems suspended. One night, lying in bed, I am woken by the loud bang of a bird flying against my window, and a word enters my sight, as if retrieved from a bricked-up wall in my tunnel of memory. *Kairos*. A word from my small portion of undergraduate Greek, a word I had stored away: meaning not time, but timeliness. By this the Greeks meant the right or opportune moment for doing, a moment that cannot be scheduled, as it is poised unpredictably between beginnings and ends. It does not submit to *chronos*, which is mere arithmetic: a minute, an hour, a day, a decade, the work of timekeepers. *Kairos* exists as a potential, a mode of improvisation, of responding to a sudden opening in the fabric of time. No theory can enable or plan for it. Abandon the fixed plan, wait for the moment to arrive, and then act. At nineteen I had been struck by this, had decided that this was how I would live my life. It seemed then to be purely a matter of resolve; instead, it requires an inhuman patience. And faith.

So this moment may never arrive, and if it arrives it may never achieve completion. Still, the potential is always there, but first you must find the place. In this place the past will be dead and the future a mirage. And when the opening appears it must be passed through without hesitation. The Greeks compared it to the moment in weaving when the shuttle can be passed through threads on the loom, the instant when a gap opens in the warp of the cloth and the weaver must draw the yarn through to make the pattern. But does this space ever exist other than in our dreams?

○

The labyrinth is almost complete.

Late one night, I hear a knock at the side door. I hesitate to get out of bed and answer it but there is always the possibility that it's Jurko and he has a problem. When I glance out the window there is no light on in his tent. Still, I should check on him. I pad woozily down the hallway and across the kitchen to unlock the door. It's Ray.

'Got a minute?' He looks uneasy.

I am reluctant to invite him in. 'It's very late, Ray. What's the problem?'

He jerks his head in the direction of the tent. 'About Jurko.'

'What about him?'

'It's bloody cold out here—can I come in or what?'

We never will like one another.

I yield, and we sit on opposite sides of the kitchen table, like adversaries in mediation.

'You might have come across my cousin Greg Stokell,' says Ray. 'The local copper.'

I had met Greg when I took some documents to the Mt Godwin police station to get my identity verified, so that I could draw money from my superannuation fund to pay Jurko.

'Greg gave me a ring tonight. Asked me if I knew about a vagrant in these parts, an illegal immigrant named Jurko.'

I stiffen. 'Just Jurko?'

'Yeah, and some bloody other wog name I didn't catch. Anyway, Greg's been contacted by the feds and asked to check him out.'

'When?'

'Said he'd drop by over the next few days.'

'And he asked you about Jurko?'

'Couldn't lie. No point. Everyone around here's seen us workin' together.'

'Have you told Jurko?'

'Can't bloody find him. He's not in his tent.'

No, often he isn't. 'I'll wait for him to come back tonight, assuming he does, and warn him.'

'Has he got a visa, one of them four-five-seven things?'

'I don't know. I've never asked.'

'You're his employer—you should know.'

'Jurko is a friend.'

'Well, he'll have to piss off pretty quickly if he hasn't. If I was him I wouldn't be showin' me face tomorrow, put it that way.'

I am distracted, and barely look at him. And then it occurs to me that he has taken my collusion for granted. 'What makes you think I won't co-operate with Greg?'

'You won't do that.' He snorts, making plain his contempt. 'You're pretty smitten with him.'

Smitten? You stupid old creep, I think: what would you know about the appetites of a woman like me? I am angry at being made to feel defensive, and just a little humiliated by this hypochondriacal toad. I give a harsh, affected laugh. 'Is that what you think, Ray? Jurko, with his dirty beard?'

'Yeah, well, I don't claim to understand women.'

'And what about you, Ray?'

'What about me?'

'Lying to Greg.'

'Not exactly. I'll just say I don't know where Jurko is. And if you move him on, quick like, I won't.' His lips tighten. 'Anyway, that'll be between me and Greg.'

'I see.'

Ray sighs, and pushes his chair back. 'Yeah, well, I'll leave yer to it.'

'Does Lynnie know about this?'

'Lynnie bloody knows everything about everyone.' He says this not with pride but with a trace of bitterness.

Yes, I think, and she goes on propping you up, though you don't deserve it.

When Ray has gone, I fold my dressing-gown around

me and wait in an armchair for Jurko to return, wait for the sound of his bike on the rough ground. It's just after one-thirty when I see the narrow funnel of light from the bike's headlamp moving steadily up the drive and I step out onto the terrace and call to him in a kind of hissing shout.

'Where have you been?'

'I go to see Amy.'

I don't believe this. First a mobile phone, then lies.

We agree that he will pack up his tent and spend the following day in my spare room and not go out while I think of how to get him away. If Greg Stokell comes I will say that Jurko has gone to the city for a few days to visit a friend. We will have to trust Ray, and Lynnie, a prospect that dismays me but appears not to faze Jurko. How on earth did you get here? I ask him, ask him at last when I might have asked him before, except that from early in our relationship we had established a truce on the subject of the past, a truce that suited me as much as it suited him.

'I crewed on a trawler boat,' he says, 'out of Jogjakarta. Illegal fishing in Australian waters.' He shrugs. 'Very common, yuh? I pay them some money and they drop me off on the coast.'

'They could have robbed you and thrown you overboard.'

'I take my chances.'

'How close to the coast did they come?'

'Close enough. The rest I swim.'

I know what the next question is: why didn't he fly in like any other tourist and apply for a temporary work visa? And then, if necessary, turn feral and overstay it, as so many do? But I know too what the likely answer is, and I don't want or need to hear it. He has a criminal record and wouldn't have been granted any kind of visa. In which case there would be no point in him holding out for an amnesty. For a time, at least, he will have to disappear, and right now I will have to find him somewhere to hide.

In the morning I ring Brian Murnane. A large house in a gentrified suburb. An antisocial owner. Where better to hide than in the big city?

All the next day Jurko stays in my back room while I bring him meals on a tray. He is agitated, and for a time paces the hallway until I insist that he return to the small brown Masonite room. Already we have packed up his things and brought them inside and later will strap them to the roof rack of the car, grateful for the heavy canopy of cloud that obscures the moon.

Somewhere in that time I offer to get him help. 'I can find you an immigration lawyer.'

'No, no lawyers. They say I am not a refugee. They say I am not from a war zone. I just go on my way. You don't worry.'

'They'll catch up with you eventually.'

He stares at the wall behind me, chewing at the nail

on his thumb, then drops his arm to his side as if overcome by fatigue. 'Yuh, well, this is a big country. First they have to find me.'

There is a hissing sound in the driveway, a loud thumping on the roof. A possum. I start, and Jurko looks at me and laughs. 'You are jumpy,' he says. 'I am the one should be jumpy.'

I turn off all the lights.

By the time we reach the freeway Jurko is asleep in the back seat while I, at the wheel, am rigidly alert. We had waited for darkness and the right time to leave the town and I had said again: I can find you an immigration lawyer. And he had repeated: *No lawyers*.

In the early morning we join the big rigs on the freeway, hulking mammoths cruising up and down their shadowy lanes. Apart from these and the occasional long-distance coach we might almost be alone. Now, on the road, the steady glare of the headlights induces in me a charmed reverie, a recollection of our last afternoon in Garra Nalla working on the labyrinth, Jurko laying the stone in a relaxed rhythm and Ray mixing the mortar. And because it was school holidays, Lexie and Jesse were there, Jesse staggering to carry the bigger stones, balancing each one against his chest and slipping over the edges of his worn thongs as he struggled to keep his balance. And Jurko accepting the stones without comment, as if it were natural that a six-year-old should work this hard, as perhaps Jurko had worked as a boy, had been expected to work. No patronising 'good boy' remarks, or 'My, how strong you are.' And I had taken my cues from Jurko, except to make pointed thanks to Jesse over lunch and produce a bag of chips, at which Jurko had given the slightest frown. And Lexie in the kitchen, making sandwiches in her languid fashion, with a vacant expression, as if her mind was somewhere else: the enigmatic vessel. And in mid-afternoon, we had sat outside in the sun around the table and eaten the scones brought over by Lynnie, and when a surfer's van pulled up beside the lagoon, blaring out a loud techno sound, Jesse had leapt from his chair and begun to dance, stamping his feet on the concrete and beating his elbows against the side of his body as if they were flapping wings, and we had all laughed, even Ray. On that afternoon the labyrinth was a world unto itself, unbound by time, a world of potential in which something might have been made whole before it was aborted by the law.

The dull cloud breaks and soon the road is wet. The rain, lit up in the headlights, blows in flurries across the bonnet of the car and the rubber on my windscreen wipers is frayed so that they give off a harsh insistent clack. I am grateful for it: they keep me awake.

Just before six, with the sky a pale grey, we cruise to a halt outside Brian's wrought-iron gates. The dawn streets are empty but for the whirring brushes and sluicing water of a street cleaner and a lone reveller slouching home from the bars and the clubs nearby. At the bottom of the street I had found an ATM and stopped to withdraw the money I owed Jurko for his labour. But still he hadn't woken and at last I had to rouse him.

Never an early riser, Brian opens the door in a dishevelled state. 'Sorry,' he says, 'the doorbell doesn't work. Have you been here long?'

We climb the stairs to the room I once shared with Daniel, all those years ago. And it's the same. Cream damask drapes, dusty now. Two single beds with yellowing white cotton quilts. A busy floral carpet in red and gold, and an Edwardian-era print of two wild stallions, one white and one black, galloping at full pelt across a stormy moor. And outside the window, the maple tree in full leaf. And here, now, in a bent loop of time, my surrogate son will lay his head.

Brian makes us a breakfast of greasy fried eggs with a crisp frill burnt black around the edges. Jurko is morose and we eat in exhausted silence while Brian potters round the kitchen in his cracked leather slippers. He asks no questions and I am grateful for his tact, though across the breakfast table he has lit up a cigarette and I wonder how long it will be before Jurko is unable to tolerate the smoke.

'Why don't you stay for a few days? Have a rest.'

My eyes are dry from fatigue, and the smoke. 'Thanks, but I have reasons to be getting back. It would look suspicious if I were away for long. I'll ring in a day or two.'

And still Jurko says nothing. But as I am leaving he

grips my arm, the first time he has touched me. His eyes are cloudy. 'This is not a good place,' he says.

'It will do for now. Brian is a good man.'

'I don't like not to finish.'

I know that he means the labyrinth. 'I'll leave it as it is and you can come back anytime you like.' I put my hand on his bony shoulder and squeeze it. 'Ring me if you run out of money.'

Brian unlocks the front door and steps out into the daylight, where he looks even more gaunt. 'I'll be in touch,' I say.

On the drive back I stop in a layby, resting my head against the driver's window to doze fitfully. I have been awake for how many hours? After a time I am roused by a giant rig thundering past, recklessly close, and I jolt into a state of wide-awake fatigue. Well, then, I might as well stop in Brockwood to buy the week's supplies, but also to collect the cast-iron fire pit I ordered two weeks earlier from the hardware store. I had told Jurko nothing about the fire pit but had intended, when the labyrinth was finished, to set it at the centre. When first I had contemplated this, Jurko had dismissed the idea with withering scorn. 'A barbecue!' he had snorted, and I had laughed. 'Not exactly, Jurko.' But had deferred to him, at first, and then ordered the fire pit from the local hardware store after searching through online catalogues: a simple three-pronged stand with a shallow circular dish.

In need of fresh air, and a walk to loosen my back, I leave the car in the CO-OP car park and walk on down to the big warehouse of second-hand furniture on the edge of the town. One of my canvas chairs has finally collapsed and I am looking for a replacement. The cavern of the warehouse is crammed with empty fridges, sagging velveteen couches, cheap sideboards, shelves of shoddy plaster lamps and Formica tables covered in motley cups, plates and glassware. But my eye is taken by a dark mass stacked against the end wall, a pile of carelessly arrayed brown wooden chairs that look like they might once have belonged to an old school. And I stand stock-still, and smile at them in a smile of recognition. Yes, of course. Some wooden chairs for the labyrinth, a rustic echo of Chartres and the perfect joke. Wearily I make an offer on three of them, three because that's all I can fit into my wagon. And in any case a trinity of chairs feels right. Tomorrow I will set them up, not across the labyrinth so that they obscure or impede it but at its centre, around the fire pit.

By the time I arrive at the shack it's dark and I turn on all the lights in the house ('this is waste'). The house does not feel empty. Outside, the labyrinth is a shadowy spiral of stone. The base has been laid but for the final section of two metres that remains boxed with timber, and the hollow henge has yet to be filled with gravel and earth. As I gaze through the window at its pattern of sinuous pathways I feel a presence, though of whom or what I couldn't say. The stonework may not be complete but the form is there, and it's the form that counts. The dream and the reality are now almost one.

The fatigue of my all-night drive lingers in the heaviness in my bones. I take some cubes of lamb out of the freezer to defrost and set the fire in the wood stove for the morning. I stand at the sink and fill a tall glass with lukewarm water, with a sense of having done this so many times before. Everything I do I have done before, and will do again—all the small things. I carry the glass to my bedroom and set it down on my bedside table. Yes, I will go to bed while I am still in this state of deep fatigue and before any of my companion ghosts can resurrect themselves in the dark. I drain the glass and turn out the light and slide into my cool bed. And sleep a deep, null sleep until, in the early morning, somewhere around five, after waking briefly to a possum on the roof, I am catapulted into a fiery dream.

I am out in a flat sunstruck suburb of some distant city and I am with my father, who is in his white doctor's coat. We are standing on the grassy verge in front of a low-slung bungalow and looking up at the sky, where a fiery machine is hurtling towards us. Just as it passes over the bungalow it collapses onto the roof and the house bursts into flame. 'Quick,' I say to Ken, 'we must go inside and rescue the baby.' But Ken demurs. 'The baby will already be dead,' he says. Stunned by his indifference I cry out and run towards the blazing house, but by the time I reach the back door the fire has burned itself out. The house is still standing, though most of the front wall is missing and the roof is barely supported and might collapse at any moment. The back door gives way with a push and to my immense joy I see the baby, a boy, lying on his change table, smiling and kicking in good health. I gather him up and hug him to me, and almost immediately see a second infant, on the floor at my feet, another child, a child I don't recognise. I kneel, and placing my own child on the floor I begin to unpin this other baby's soiled napkin, and as I go about it Ken arrives. Clutching both infants, one in each arm, I wander among the broken furniture to assess the damage. A pigeon flies in through the collapsed front wall and again I become agitated, and beseech my father to find a net to trap it in: we cannot leave the bird to shit all over the house, I say. I am looking around at my possessions, framed pictures blackened with soot, blue and white porcelain on shelves, small jewels in cupboard drawers, and I see that there is really nothing here that I value. I will take the children and leave the house to the insurers. They will give me money and I will start again somewhere else. In short order my feelings have changed from terror to resignation, to hope for something better. Clutching the children I rush from the house and out into the street, where a man is standing on the verge, a man in a dark suit. He turns and beckons me towards him and I see that it's my brother, Axel. Of course, I think: it would be you.

o

Two days have passed. I am about to make my first coffee when I hear a knock at the door. It's the local police sergeant, Greg Stokell.

'Mrs Marsden? Mrs Erica Marsden?'

'Yes.'

'Sorry to disturb you early.'

'That's okay.' He is taking me in, making an assessment. Whatever Ray has told him about me it wouldn't have been flattering.

'I am enquiring after the whereabouts of one Jurko Wolfgang Lazovic.'

'Yes, well, we'd all like to know where Jurko is.'

'When did you last see him?'

'Four days ago. He went to his tent in the evening and I haven't seen him since.'

'And you've no idea where he might have gone?'

'No.' I have not invited him in.

'Nothing he said?'

'No.'

He jerks his head in the direction of the labyrinth. 'He hasn't finished the job, has he?'

'No, he's let me down. But then, he's very eccentric. I knew he was a risk when I took him on.'

'He's an illegal immigrant.'

'I had no idea.'

I can see that Greg doesn't believe me. Can see also that he doesn't care. He is playing his part and I am playing mine. It's a steady minuet: one step forward and

238

two steps back.

'Well, if you hear anything, let me know.'

'Of course.'

I have at least learned one thing, Jurko's surname. The name of the father. I had asked him once but he wouldn't tell me. 'I renounce this name. I am just Jurko.'

○

Daniel has grown his hair. Not long, but his thick black curls have reappeared, cropped in coils and streaked with grey. He is lost to me now, more than ever. No longer his mother's angry captive. Never mind. To me he will always be the boy who drew in the margins of books.

'Your books, Daniel. There are still so many to burn.'

'Don't trouble yourself, Ma. Give them away.'

It's a long time since he called me Ma.

The warder is tapping his boot against the floor. Tap, tap, in a dead beat.

'If you are sure.' I will sell them and give the money to Lexie to add to her savings.

He nods.

'I would like a drawing. If you have one to spare.' I have given nothing away, nothing of Jodie's intelligence. If he gives me a portrait of Roger Kemp I will burn it.

'Perhaps later.' He smiles a condescending smile.

I turn to look at the mural on the wall behind me, the muddy orange-brown trees daubed with thick green streaks. 'You could apply to repaint that,' I say. 'To paint over it, I mean.'

'I already have.'

'Really? What did they say?'

'They're thinking about it.'

'Do you have anything in mind, Daniel?'

The same faint smile. 'Not yet.'

The warder coughs. I look up and he points to the clock on the wall.

Daniel stands and folds his hands in front of him, like a cleric about to deliver a homily. 'Kiss me, Ma.'

I rise, and placing a hand on his shoulder to steady myself I put my lips to the stubble on his cheek.

That night my phone rings and I see that it's Brian.

'Is it Jurko?' I ask.

'He's gone.' A deep sigh. 'Shot through.'

'Did he say anything before he left?'

'Nothing. I got up this morning and found a note on the kitchen table. *Thank you, Brian.*'

'That's all?'

'That's all. Only he spelled it B-r-i-n-e.'

'I can't say I'm surprised. But thanks, Brian—thanks for everything.'

'I might come and see you one weekend. When it's not so hot.'

'Yes, do.'

I look for Jurko's phone number in my Contacts but when I ring, the number is disconnected.

o

In the morning I ring Diana and invite her down for dinner. Tonight I will light the fire pit. I will mix cocktails and we will sit on the brown chairs and eat and I will make a small ceremony of this.

But for now I am restless, febrile with fatigue, and I set out on a walk along the road that leads to the lagoon. Spume from the surf is rising in a fine haze and the air shimmers. The weeds in the rocky swales beside the road are wilting in the glare and the grassy verge is bleached dry. I am aching in every bone, but alert and hyper-observant, like an animal sprung from its trap.

At the water's edge I sit on a rocky ledge by a thicket of boobialla and contemplate the surfers, black-suited figures bobbing up and down in the incoming swell. In their wait to catch a wave they are patient, and the surge of the swell is hypnotic so that soon I am patient with them, until a lumbering march fly appears from nowhere to hover at my shoulder. I look up, and see two tall men walking towards me, and as they approach I recognise the older one. It's Lewis Eames, with a younger man beside him.

'Erica.'

'Lewis.' I stand and make to walk on but he stops, blocking my path, and lays a hand on the young man's shoulder. 'This is my son, Caleb.'

'Really.' The young man is eager and leans forward, as if he recognises me. 'How long are you here for, Caleb?'

'Just a few days. Are you the woman who built the labyrinth?'

'Yes.'

'I'd love to see it. I'm a landscape gardener and they're becoming popular now.'

'Are they?'

'Yes, as a garden feature, mostly. Though some farmers are cutting big ones into crops as a draw for visitors.'

'So have you installed one?'

'Not yet.'

Caleb's eyes are soft and unguarded, and I see that he does not yet share in the disappointments of his father. 'Well, come by in the morning if you'd like.' I look to Lewis and raise my eyebrows. 'You can come too, Lewis.'

Lewis nods. 'I may just do that.'

'But not before eleven.' And I smile at Caleb, who steps aside so that I can pass.

At the turning circle on the road above, a big SUV is disgorging its occupants. They leap out onto the dusty bitumen with their dogs and begin to unstrap their boards from the roof rack while the dogs wheel and frolic in the loose gravel. A second car pulls in, trailing a cloud of dust, and I turn away from the road and head down to the narrow track that runs beside the marsh where the black swans build their nests. In the morning, then: Caleb. Always the same story: someone else's son.

o

By late afternoon the air has cooled and I gather sticks to build a neat pyre, set with thin logs from my woodpile and planted with small white cubes of kerosene firelighters that nestle between newspaper and kindling. The grass all around is dry again and I must be careful: sparks could fly off into the dunes or land in the paddocks.

By the time Diana arrives the fire is a mound of glowing coals. I indicate the wooden chairs, on one of which is a tray of drinks. When we are both seated, Diana looks around her with the air of an inspector on official business.

'Why the fire pit?'

'I considered a pizza oven but decided against it.'

'Honestly, Erica, you're a strange woman.'

'Not all that strange.'

'In summer there'll be a fire ban and you won't be able to use it.'

'Then it can function as a bird bath.'

Diana leans back in her chair and runs her hands through her dark cropped hair, looking around at the low stone walls of the labyrinth. 'Are you going to finish this thing?'

'Maybe.'

'Where's Jurko? His tent's not there.'

'He's gone.'

'Gone where?'

'Good question.'

'I warned you, didn't I? I said he'd be unreliable.'

'You did.'

'You don't seem to mind.'

'Ray has offered to finish it for me.'

'Has he now?'

'I told him I'd wait and see if Jurko came back.'

'You don't want Ray around, do you?'

'No.'

'What if Jurko doesn't come back?'

I shrug.

'Doesn't it bother you that it's not finished?'

'No, not really.' Yes, it does, it does bother me, but unthinkable that anyone other than Jurko should complete it.

We sit now in the companionable silence that of late has come easily to us. Overhead a formation of swans is flying home towards the marshes and Diana looks up, yawns and straightens her back. 'Come down to the lagoon tomorrow. Could be the last swim of the season.'

'You think?'

'The warm current is moving further south. It won't be long before the water gets cold and you haven't got a wetsuit.'

'I'm not a wetsuit person.'

But Diana isn't listening; she is gazing out beyond the sandhills. 'Look at that.'

'What?'

The moon, a deep-pink sphere, has risen over the sea and sits low above the horizon. A thin vertical band of charcoal cloud has drifted across its surface to bisect it, so neatly that the effect is of two halves suspended in perfect symmetry.

She stands, and picks up a stick to poke at the coals. 'I like your fire pit.'

'So do I.'

'It will be good in autumn.'

'It will.'

'And now I'll have to be careful not to bust my shins on your henge.'

Together we stroll down the long sandy driveway to the road where Diana's van is parked on the verge. By now it is almost dark, and as I walk back along the drive towards the house the small solar lights planted in the sand begin to flare. At the garden tap I fill a ceramic pitcher with water and carry it across to the fire pit to douse the coals. Yesterday was my mother's birthday, and by now Irene would be eighty-nine. Her face is beyond imagining, indeed I can barely recall the fragile image of it that I carried with me as a child. And so here is her labyrinth, its opening curves the nub of the cervix, its outer wall the lining of the womb. And at its centre, the iron fire pit. *Labrys*: the womb and the axe.

Tomorrow is the second Thursday of the month, and in the morning I will rise early and set out to visit Daniel. But now the light above the hills has darkened, and without the glow of the fire I must tread carefully between the stone walls of the henge and make my way back to the house.

There, at the open door, pitcher in hand, I turn to look again at the spiral, now barely discernible in the dusk. The fugue is ended, and I will go inside and ring my brother.

At the other end of the phone there is silence, the silence of a deep indrawn breath. And then: 'Good God, Erica. Is that you?'